PENGUIN CRIME FICTION

LAUGHTER IN THE ALEHOUSE

Henry Kane, creator of the best-selling Peter
Chambers series, introduced the urbane
McGregor in *The Midnight Man,* a tale of
murder in the glittering upper reaches of
Manhattan's loan-shark aristocracy. *Conceal
and Disguise* exposed the former New York
police inspector to the chilly winds of the
cold war. *Laughter in the Alehouse* re-
soundingly confirms McGregor's rank in the
upper echelons of detective fiction.

Laughter in the Alehouse

BY HENRY KANE

PENGUIN BOOKS

Penguin Books Ltd, Harmondsworth,
Middlesex, England
Penguin Books, 625 Madison Avenue,
New York, New York 10022, U.S.A.
Penguin Books Australia Ltd, Ringwood,
Victoria, Australia
Penguin Books Canada Limited, 2801 John Street,
Markham, Ontario, Canada L3R 1B4
Penguin Books (N.Z.) Ltd, 182–190 Wairau Road,
Auckland 10, New Zealand

First published in the United States of America as
A Cock Robin Mystery by The Macmillan Company 1968
First published in Canada by
Collier-Macmillan Canada Limited 1968
Published in Penguin Books 1978

LIBRARY OF CONGRESS CATALOGING IN PUBLICATION DATA
Kane, Henry.
Laughter in the alehouse.
Reprint of the 1968 ed. published by Macmillan,
New York, in series: A Cock robin mystery.
I. Title.
[PZ3.K1318Lau 1978]   813'.5'4   78-2248
ISBN 0 14 00.4936 3

Printed in the United States of America by
Offset Paperback Mfrs., Inc., Dallas, Pennsylvania
Set in Times Roman

℞ One

GIDEON RABIN was the first assistant to the consul general in New York City, but the car he was driving was not equipped with diplomatic license plates. It was a station wagon owned by his wife and registered in her name, Aliza Rabin, and he was driving his wife's car because, although the business was important, it was not official business.

In the morning sunlight, in his wife's car, Gideon Rabin lit a cigarette and sighed. It was a good thing, he thought, that the consul general was back home on his once-a-year sixty-day vacation. He sighed again, guiltily, and tossed the just-begun cigarette out the open window. No, it would have made no difference. He would have been embarked on this selfsame enterprise—except with the consul general in residence the situation might have proved awkward. *Proved* awkward? Hell, it *was* awkward, and he had no one to blame but himself.

He glanced sidelong at the newspapers on the passenger's seat beside him—yesterday's evening papers and today's morning papers—each containing the item of news as promised. He scowled, repressed a shudder. He plucked out another cigarette, used the car-lighter to ignite it. He inhaled deeply, flung the cigarette out the window. It was simply too damn early for tobacco. He had not yet had breakfast. He drove through the cool clear June morning toward Kennedy International Airport.

He was far ahead of schedule: the traffic had been heavy the other way, coming into the city; going out, toward the airport, it had been nothing, a trickle. It was seven-thirty and the plane was not due until eight. Good. Better than good. Excellent. He could fortify himself. Food. He was hungry: the crisp morning air had given him an appetite. He had until eight o'clock, even more if there were a delay. He shrugged: it did not figure for any delay. It would be a government jet with a full crew, but only one passenger. He knew. Yagid himself had told him.

In the restaurant he ordered juice, oatmeal with cream, a toasted bran muffin. He ate swiftly and then, over coffee, for the first time that morning, enjoyed his cigarette. Half-smiling, he shook his head—an enormous jet plane with a full crew and only one passenger. He even knew the amount of the baggage. Three trunks. Yagid had told him.

He was beginning to feel better. His belly was assuaged, the cigarette was good, the coffee delicious. He was in deep, but not so deep that he could not get out. He had acted in good faith—in his opinion it was an emergency matter—but good faith was no excuse for a diplomatic breach. If the facts were revealed he could be recalled and Aliza would hate that and so would he: they loved being here in the United States, loved New York City. Yet he had climbed all the way out on a limb, and Aliza, approvingly, had climbed with him. He smoked his cigarette, sipped coffee. He was a part of the diplomatic corps, not cloak-and-dagger, not a spy or a counterspy or anything like that, and such involvement could subject him to recall. He shook his head. The damn thing had started four days ago—today was the fifth day —and it had started as normal routine at the consulate. The lady had wanted to see the man in charge.

His secretary, skillful at screening, had nevertheless shown her through, a petite, rather attractive woman in her middle thirties, Anna Stryker. But when Miss Stryker had expressed the purpose of her visit, Mr. Rabin had feigned interest but felt boredom. Another individual, a generation later, come to report another hidden Nazi war criminal. Over the years they had had them by the scores, in consulates and embassies all over the world, almost always malcontents with hate or a grudge or an ax to grind. There were very few wanted war criminals extant; as compared to the constant flow of complaints and reports from the malcontents, there were virtually none. Most had already been apprehended, the rest were dead. Still there were a number alive and unarrested, a minuscule number, and so Gideon Rabin heard the woman out, perfunctorily making notes.

2

He took down her name, address, phone number. She was in New York only ten days, from Sydney, Australia. Her one next of kin was a sister, Miss Gertrude Stryker, living on Long Island. She was here to report about a man named Konrad Kassel, she had proof positive of his criminality. Rabin did not press for details; he had neither the art nor the experience. That would be the province of a Shinbet agent, skilled in interrogation, who could separate wheat from chaff. He told her that such an agent would, in short order, be in touch with her, terminated the interview, promptly transmitted the information to Tel Aviv and Jerusalem, and another minor routine job was finished for him. Or so he thought.

The next night, at home, he received the call from Yagid. Yagid himself. Oscar Yagid, chief of Sherutei Bion, colloquially Shinbet, the CIA of Israel. Yagid had instructed him to keep Miss Stryker available, informed him that Juliette Gaza was being detached from West Berlin to handle the investigation. Yagid told him when, where, and how Miss Gaza would arrive, and that Rabin, personally, was to meet her. Another agent, Dave Jordan, was being recalled from Buenos Aires to assist Miss Gaza. Jordan would call the consulate and tell Rabin of his whereabouts in the city, which information Rabin would pass on to Miss Gaza. When Gideon Rabin, perspiring, had hung up, he was aware that whatever it was, however meager, he had gleaned from Anna Stryker, it had pricked a nerve at Israeli intelligence. Were not the matter of paramount importance, an underling rather than Yagid himself would have called (or there would have been no call at all: in the many prior instances of similar circumstance Shinbet, properly, had assumed jurisdiction without further communication with the consulate). And were not the matter of paramount importance, Juliette Gaza—intramural of tremendous reputation, a most formidable secret agent—Juliette Gaza would not have been selected for the assignment. Rabin had met Miss Gaza only once, six years ago, in Bonn, at the reception for the Chancellor of West Germany. He had never heard of Dave Jordan, but that, he assured himself, was par for the course. Gaza had been the exception, Jordan the norm. The Shinbet agents of Israel, like the CIA agents of America, were unknown to the constituted authorities and frequently unknown to one another. Par for the course. Why should Gideon

Rabin know about Dave Jordan? Rabin was attached to the embassy, the consulate, to officialdom; the people of Shinbet were apart, alone, sole.

Rather humbly the next afternoon, at twelve o'clock of the third day, he had called Anna Stryker. No answer. He had called every half hour until six o'clock. No answer. Then, quitting the office but first phoning Aliza he would be delayed, he had made a visit to 523 East 47th Street, Anna Stryker's address.

It was an old house, a walkup; her apartment was up a steep stairway to the first floor, 1C, at the head of the stairs. He rang to no reply, went down to the super on the ground floor to inquire, and was told. Miss Stryker had met with a bad accident. At about eleven o'clock that morning, the super had been roused by the sound of a frightful crash. Rushing out of his apartment he had found Miss Stryker at the foot of the stairway, unconscious, bleeding from the head. Quite obviously she had tripped and gone down the whole way. The super, unable to stem the flow of blood or revive the woman, had called for an ambulance, and she was now in Bellevue Hospital. Discreetly, Rabin had checked the hospital. The woman was in the public ward. She had had no visitors.

At home, morose, he had passed up dinner, pleading headache and an upset stomach. After Aliza had gone to bed, he had tried to watch television but could not concentrate. His mind remained with Anna Stryker, his imagination turning tricks. The woman, without vestige of doubt, was a concern to the people of Shinbet. Yagid had said to keep her available, and special agents were being flown in. Something she had said, of the little he had permitted her to say, had rung a bell at the headquarters of Sherutei Bion. Was it coincidence that she had met with accident the day after reporting to the consulate? Had she fallen down that flight of stairs or—had she been pushed? In short, was she the victim of a murder attempt? He considered calling Yagid and informing him, but hesitated. He was inexperienced in affairs of cloak-and-dagger. Wires could be tapped—on this end or the other. Within thirty-six hours the Shinbet agents would be here, and it would be out of his hands. In the meantime, for that short interval, it was up to him. It was his baby.

He had gone to bed, could not sleep. At two o'clock he woke

Aliza. In the kitchen over coffee he told her, and she was most sympathetic. "In the morning," she had said. "There's nothing we can do now. It'll keep until morning." It had been good. Confession was catharsis. He was able to sleep.

And so on the morning of the fourth day he had called the hospital, inquired, learned the woman's condition was the same and that she still had had no visitors. He had checked the Long Island telephone books for a Miss Gertrude Stryker, found none. Not unusual: people have unlisted numbers. He had consulted with Aliza and come to a decision. If someone *had* attempted the murder of Anna Stryker, let that someone believe he had been successful.

He had called in Dr. Leo Vernon, his personal physician. He had advised him of some of the facts, but not all. He had stressed the possibility of the murder attempt, informed him that the woman might be the nub of an important international affair. He had pleaded that the woman needed expert medical attention and that Vernon was the man to afford that attention. He had convinced the doctor and they had used a private ambulance.

At the hospital Aliza, posing as the sister of the stricken woman, had signed her out, and it had gone without untoward incident. Overcrowded hospitals are not loath to be rid of unscheduled patients. Rabin had paid the fees, and Vernon had noted the history and taken over the patient. Anna Stryker was in poor condition but not critical. A laceration on the right side of her forehead had required nine stitches and she had suffered a concussion of the brain. She was in a semicoma, under sedation, and being fed intravenously. The ambulance had brought her to the Rabin apartment and there she was ensconced in the guest room, the extra bedroom, under the care of Dr. Vernon and with Aliza as her nurse.

That had been the beginning, but not the end. If murder had been attempted, the murderer had to be lulled, and to that effect Rabin went to the office of Bill Brundidge, a powerful public relations man, a personal friend, and, for all his bulk and years, a romantic. The Israeli consulate in New York City was one of Bill Brundidge's permanent clients.

"Bill," Rabin had begun when they were alone, "I have a matter for you of utmost secrecy but importance." He had told some truths and some half-truths, exciting and inciting Brundidge to the action required. "I want it in the papers," Rabin said, "all the papers. That the woman is dead. No headlines, of course, she's not *that* important. We believe someone tried to kill her and we want that someone to believe he did. If it turns out to be a mistake— well, you were mistaken. You've got enough pull with the papers to plant it. They won't check. I repeat, she's not that important. Just an item. Out of respect to the dead, sort of a public notice, an item that the woman died as a result of her accident. Bill, you've got the know-how, the connections. We'll be eternally grateful. . . ."

"I'll see what I can do," Brundidge had said.

And he had done it. The item had appeared in the evening papers of that fourth day and now in the morning papers of the fifth day. Each folded to that specific page, the items circled in pencil, the newspapers lay on the passenger's seat of Aliza's station wagon.

He finished the coffee, stubbed out the cigarette. His hand was trembling. Hell, it had been a nerve-wracking few days. He was a diplomat, dammit, not some kind of skulking spy.

He looked at his watch, ten minutes to eight, and consoled himself that soon now, imminently, it would be out of his hands and in the hands of the experts. He motioned for the check, paid, quit the restaurant, waited impatiently outside Customs, and at a quarter after eight Juliette Gaza emerged.

Beautiful. Nerves or no, he chuckled. Forgive me, Aliza. I am old but not so old I cannot appreciate pulchritude. Tall and shapely. Red hair and brown eyes. An exceedingly beautiful young woman. Young? Perhaps not. Who knows? Ageless.

She recognized him immediately and came forward, immaculate in a white form-fitting suit, smiling.

"Mr. Rabin."

"Welcome, Miss Gaza."

They shook hands.

☙ Two

THE three trunks firmly emplaced in the rear of the station wagon and his passenger, having graciously taken the folded newspapers into her lap, sitting beside him, Gideon Rabin maneuvered the car out of Kennedy Airport. He had much to say but said nothing. These people, he admitted to himself, in a sense frightened him. They were special people in a special world of their own. They were real—there she sat, flesh and blood—but somehow they were unreal and they inhibited him. It was the lady who breached the silence.

"Have you had word from Dave Jordan?"

"Yes." He was stammering. "He—he called in yesterday. He's staying at the Chelsea Hotel. On Twenty-third Street."

"Good. And the woman?"

"Yes, er, the woman. The newspapers you're holding. Please look, Miss Gaza. The news items I've encircled."

She looked and he heard her gasp.

"No," he said.

"My dear God!"

"Not dead," he said, and told his story, and then breathlessly, "Fools—and amateurs—rush in where angels fear to tread. I rushed, Miss Gaza. Perhaps a fool, certainly an amateur. But in the circumstances, I—in a manner of speaking, I was constrained. I hope I haven't messed matters." He laughed nervously. "My boss'll have my head."

"Excellent. My dear sir, absolutely excellent. No professional could have done better, and nobody will have your head, I assure you. Quite the contrary. You're to be commended, and you shall be. May I be the first."

"Pardon?"

"To commend you."

"Oh." Fumbling, shyly. "Thank you."

"Again, contrary. I—better the plural, we—thank *you*, Mr. Rabin. When may I talk with her?"

"I'm afraid at present she's in no condition for talking, but you'll discuss it with the doctor. He'll be in to see her at nine-thirty. We have time, first, to get you settled in your hotel."

"The Delmonico."

"Yes, Yagid told me."

In the city Rabin supervised as the porter brought the trunks to her suite. Lavish. Shinbet was lavish with important operatives and Miss Juliette Gaza was an important operative. There were two bedrooms, two bathrooms, a pantry, a copious kitchen, a superb sitting room, and wall-to-wall carpeting throughout, including the bathrooms. The trunks delivered into one bedroom, Miss Gaza freshened in the other, and then Rabin drove her to his home, a penthouse apartment on the same street as the consulate, East 70th Street.

He introduced her to Aliza and to Dr. Leo Vernon.

"May I talk with her, Doctor?"

"Impossible, Miss Gaza."

"Urgent, Doctor. Believe me."

"I believe you. Impossible, Miss Gaza."

"That bad?"

"Not too bad, really. She's had her lumps, the poor woman. Getting along. Improving. But she's in no shape for talk. Simply wouldn't comprehend."

"When?"

"Gideon told you?"

"Yes he did."

"The cut on her head, normal. Healing normally. Concussion is another matter; concussion is tricky. Not bad, not too bad, she'll come around. A day or two. Three. A week at the outside."

"You'll inform me immediately? I mean when she can talk? Comprehend?"

"I'll tell Gideon. He'll tell you."

"Yes, Doctor. May I see her?"

"Why not?" He led her to a bedroom.

The woman lay supine, her head propped on two pillows. Her eyes were closed, her face flushed. A wide strip of adhesive tape was thick on the right side of her forehead. Her lips were bloodless, pale, parted, and she was breathing through her mouth—deep, long, rattling gasps. The room was pleasantly cool but there was a fetid odor. Juliette Gaza tiptoed out, followed by the doctor.

"God, she looks terrible."

"She's an ill woman, Miss Gaza."

"Doctor, if she dies. . . ."

"She won't."

"Doctor, I tell you, I *must* talk to her."

"You will. In time."

"Doctor, I tell you, if there's any chance that she *will* die . . . before . . ."

For one quick moment Dr. Leo Vernon thought he had another patient for sedation. The beautiful young woman had her hands tightly clenched. She stood tall, jaw rigid, eyes blazing. "Doctor, it's imperative that I talk with her. Please don't be kind with me. If you have any doubt whatever that she will survive—then you must do something at once. Revive her, by whatever means. I *must* talk with her."

"She'll live."

"Doctor. . . ."

"I'm the doctor, Miss Gaza."

Silence, the woman's eyes burning into his. Then, meekly, she said, "Yes, Doctor," and turned from him and went to the other room, to Gideon Rabin. "Is there a phone, please? Where I may be alone?"

"This way."

He led her to the phone and she called Information for the number of the Chelsea Hotel; then dialed it.

"Mr. Jordan, please."

"Do you know the room number?"

"No."

"One moment, please."

There were clickings from the switchboard, then the buzz-ringing of the phone at the other end, then a deep baritone.

"Jordan here."

"Juliette Gaza."

"Ah. Good to have you."

She felt herself frown. "Beg pardon?"

"Good to have you here in the States, Miss Gaza."

"Are you free?"

"For you, of course."

"I'm staying at the Delmonico. Suite Fourteen Hundred. Can you be there in half an hour?"

"I'm at your service."

"Half hour?"

"You got me, Miss Gaza."

He hung up and she stood contemplating the handset, then slowly returned it to its cradle. A brief conversation but peculiarly pregnant. Filled with double entendre, or had she imagined? She wondered what he looked like. His voice was vibrant, assured, somewhat cocky, tinged with humor, thoroughly American. She experienced a thrill of prescience, shook it off but smiled: even the most dreadful assignment could have, as a tangent, a pleasant aspect. She tapped a fingernail against the telephone, then shrugged, turned, went quickly to the living room, to Gideon and Aliza Rabin and Dr. Leo Vernon.

"Miss Gaza," Aliza Rabin said, "will you stay and have a bit of breakfast with us? Al fresco, on the terrace. It's a beautiful morning."

"Not me," Gideon Rabin said. "I've had breakfast. Got to go to work."

"Then with Dr. Vernon and myself?"

"No, thank you. I must get back to the hotel."

"I'll take you," Rabin said.

"Please don't bother."

"No bother at all."

"A beautiful woman." Aliza sighed. "His one weakness—beautiful women."

"Which is why I chose you as the permanent companion, my dear."

"Isn't he delightful? We'll be married thirty years come September and I must say never once has he failed to say the right thing at the right time."

"A diplomat," said Dr. Vernon. "That's his business."

"A remark," said Rabin, "which proves that *you're* no diplomat."

"I'm a doctor," said the doctor.

"Yes, doctor. Come along, Miss Gaza."

"Thank you all," said Miss Gaza, "for everything."

"Gideon, when this thing, whatever it is, is over, you'll bring Miss Gaza again. We'll have a party."

"Sure," said Rabin.

"Yes, Miss Gaza?"

"Certainly," said Miss Gaza.

In the station wagon, on the short trip to the Delmonico, she asked, "Yagid mentioned Holzer?"

"Yes."

"He's available?"

"Oh yes."

"We'll want to talk to him."

"I know."

"Today, quite possibly."

"Whenever you say."

"Either Dave Jordan or myself."

"You'll tell me. You're the boss. I'll be at the consulate all day."

"You've been very kind, Mr. Rabin."

"Duty," he said.

"Far and beyond the call of duty."

"Well, thank you." He grinned. He had fine white teeth, not his. At his age, not his. American dentists, she thought. The best.

"The consul general," she said. "He has lovely teeth."

"Teeth? What?" Perplexity wrinkled his eyes.

"American dentists," she said. "Wonderful."

"Dentists?"

"The consul general, he's old."

"Young."

"Sixty-eight."

"Young. Vital. Full, as they say here, of pep. Peppy. On the ball. In all his faculties."

"January One, he's recalled. His own request. He's retiring. Do you know that, Mr. Rabin?"

"How do you know, Miss Gaza?"

"We at Shinbet know. Do you?"

"Yes. Confidential."

"You're next in line, Mr. Rabin."

"I, and many others."

"Do you want it, Mr. Rabin?"

The car stopped at a red light. His face turned to hers. "I don't understand the question."

"Simple. Do you want it?"

"Yes." The light turned green.

"You've got it, Mr. Consul General. As of January One, you're it."

"But . . . but. . . ."

"You're perfectly qualified, you're the man. They gave it to Yagid for recommendation and Yagid gave it to me, a part of my work here. Well, at least that work is done; quickly, but my best judgment. You're it. Don't blush. Finished."

"May I—tell Aliza?"

"Of course." And now she grinned. "But confidential."

The station wagon stopped in front of the Delmonico. Juliette Gaza got out and leaned in through the aperture of the rolled-down window. "You'll let me know when I can talk with Anna Stryker?"

"Vernon says it won't be for several days."

"You'll let me know immediately?"

"Immediately."

"You did a hell of a good job on that, you and your wife. I thank you, Yagid thanks you, your consul general thanks you." She leaned in all the way, reached her hands to his face, pulled him to her and kissed his cheek.

℘ Three

UPSTAIRS she first fixed in a mirror and then, while waiting for Jordan, opened one of the trunks and took out a large, string-and-button manila file. It was stamped KONRAD MANNHEIM, NE KONRAD KASSEL. She brought it to the sitting room and there, glancing again in a mirror, laid the file on a table and stood in front of the mirror, debating whether or not to remove the jacket of her suit. With it on she looked far too formal for receiving a guest in home surroundings. But with it off. . . .

She removed the jacket. Her blouse was sleeveless, rather sheer, provocatively filled. She smiled at her reflection in the mirror, noted the mischief in her eyes. She was fully aware of her hour-glass-type figure and of male reaction to its curves and dimensions. She pirouetted, made the full turn, laughed aloud. Why not? She remembered the deep masculine voice, the subtle insouciance, the cheerful American accent, and suddenly wondered whether *he* had wondered about *her* accent. She spoke German and Hebrew and had a smattering of Yiddish, but her education had been in England and her accent was definitely British. Had he wondered about her? Ruefully she had to admit that she had about him, but only after their brief conversation on the phone. Somehow—she sighed—it had excited her. Before that, nothing: he was another cog in the intricate machinery, another of the multitude of international agents. Yagid had told her he was a native-born New Yorker who had once lived in Madrid and spoke fluent Spanish, which was why he had drawn the Buenos Aires assignment.

She hung away the jacket and returned to business. First, from the manila file she drew out the many photographs, full-lengths and close-ups, quite recently taken. Distinguished. Tall, erect,

13

rapier-slim. Handsome. An interesting face: narrow eyes, thin lips, gray temples, a pointed chin, an aquiline nose, a clean jaw, no flab; a face like a fox. And from the file she extracted the clipped-together sheaf of papers and reviewed the closely-typed data.

Konrad Kassel. Now in America, having taken on his mother's maiden name, known as Konrad Mannheim. Konrad Kassel, son and sole progeny of the notorious SS General Wilhelm von Kassel, master of the massacres at Auschwitz. Auschwitz, in the province of Cracow in the country of Poland, where 4,000,000 Jews had been exterminated—4,000,000 living, breathing, normal, hoping, hopeful, busy, involved human beings—done to death by gas, fire, phenol injection, shooting, hanging, inquisition, torture, experimentation. And the supervisor of this holocaust was SS General Wilhelm von Kassel, second in command of the entire area.

She sighed deeply, continued with her reading.

Auschwitz, dread name, a pinpoint in history, but in fact a vast terrain. The concentration camp of Birkenau was the crematory, but the fodder was supplied from the thirty slave-labor camps surrounding it, and the commander of Camp No. 6 had been SS Colonel Konrad Kassel, the son of General Wilhelm von Kassel. The colonel had shuttled 60,000 souls to incineration at Birkenau, but had remained free of criminal stigma. He had not known, or so it was said. Until the very last days he had not known; that had been the judgment at Nuremberg. When in those last days he had learned, he had denounced the general and in the fury of recrimination had shot him—the son had murdered the father.

It was possible he had not known: Auschwitz was a vast complex. He had believed—so he had said—that transfers from Camp No. 6 to Birkenau had been just that: routine transfers. His statements had been supported by the testimony of three witnesses, Jewish prisoners certainly not biased in his favor—Benjamin Jankowski, Jacob Stryker, and Alfred Holzer—who had heard the son's denunciation of the father and had witnessed the resultant heat of passion murder.

Konrad Kassel. As a youth he had dropped the aristocratic "von" from the middle of his name. Scion of a military family, he

14

had been a rather romantic figure in those dear dead days long ago. His education at Heidelberg had been interrupted by the Great War, and at nineteen he was already a decorated ace of the Luftwaffe, and had risen in commission until at twenty-three he was a full colonel. In 1945, at age twenty-four, he had been transferred to Auschwitz and established as commander of Camp No. 6. He had served only two months and the war had ended—but during that final furious period 60,000 Jews had passed from Camp No. 6 to the ovens of Birkenau. It was possible—barely but within the realm of possibility—that the youthful SS Colonel Konrad Kassel had in fact been an innocent spared of the truth, a dupe of the father. That testimony was to this day uncontroverted.

He had come to America, taken the name Konrad Mannheim, and was president of Mannheim Incorporated, which he owned, a small, fairly prosperous import business with offices at 277 Park Avenue in New York, and in the interests of his business he traveled extensively. His file, closed these many years, had rather recently been opened because Kassel/Mannheim had finally surfaced.

In Buenos Aires the National Socialist League of Argentina was beyond doubt the richest organization of its type in the world, flourishing by virtue of its alleged militant anti-communist precepts. It was in fact at the other extreme of the totalitarian spectrum, the world nucleus of the new fascism, and it had been discovered, rather recently, that Konrad Mannheim was one of its active constituents.

In Germany, in West Berlin, the *Blau Gruppe*—the Blue Group—powerful in the new politics, was at the core of the proliferating neo-Nazism. Its aims were the unification of Germany (popular), acquisition of nuclear armaments (popular), annihilation, even by war, of the communism of Red Russia and Red China (fairly popular), and eventual elimination of the non-Aryans, the Jews and the jungle-Blacks of the world (not yet unanimously popular). The germinating jackboot philosophy of the *Blau Gruppe,* laughed off by young people as another insane shoot of another extremist group, was not laughed off by oldsters like Yagid who remembered. And a man named Konrad Mannheim, a businessman in the United States, was slated to quit America, return permanently to Germany, and take over as

Fuehrer of *Blau Gruppe;* Kassel/Mannheim, valiant, vaunted, devoted, cloaked within the secrecy of the convoluted layers of free enterprise—the indefatigable, peripatetic Konrad the Fox, powerfully supported, would be put up for election as Chancellor of the German Federal Republic. And so months ago Oscar Yagid, in pursuance of the new inquiry into Konrad Kassel/Mannheim, had assigned Dave Jordan to Buenos Aires and Juliette Gaza to West Berlin.

The ring of the telephone startled Juliette Gaza, engrossed. She put away the papers, picked up the phone. "Yes?"

"I'm downstairs."

"Pardon?"

"Dave Jordan. On the house-phone in the lobby. Okay for me to come up?"

"Oh yes. Please."

౭ Four

WHEN the knock came she opened the door and her heart simultaneously soared and plummeted, a paradox. There he stands in my doorway too damned beautiful vis-à-vis my admitted vulnerability. Dear God, this would be a man to meet at a splendid ball during a gay vacation. What in hell has Yagid sent me as my partner in deadly serious work?

A gleaming, shining man. Very tall. Dark. Black hair, curly, careless. A straight nose, a hard chin, a blue jaw, and bold black eyes, patently appreciative, casually appraising her.

"Miss Gaza?"

"Juliette Gaza."

"Dave Jordan." He took her hand, tiny in his, squeezed it gently.

16

"Please come in."

He moved with a loose, easy gait. He had long legs and wide shoulders, and now as he came very close she could see the laughwrinkles in the corners of his eyes. He moved with grace; strikingly handsome, not a boy, perhaps in his late thirties, lean, lithe, he came all the way and stood tall above her, their bodies almost touching, and bruskly, angrily, defensively she said, "Do you know why you're here, Mr. Jordan?"

"People I like call me Dave." The deep voice had a mocking overtone.

The bastard. Am I so much the little girl, transparent? Damn you, Yagid. She moved a step away from him, her legs stiff.

"Do you know why you're here, Mr. Jordan?"

He shrugged, took a folded yellow paper from a pocket. He was wearing black slacks and a brown tweed jacket. A pink sports shirt, tieless, was open at the neck. He handed her the paper, stood watching as she opened it. It was Yagid's cable.

RETURN NEW YORK IMMEDIATELY. REPORT RABIN
AT CONSULATE. GAZA WILL CONTACT. YAGID.

She folded the cablegram, gave it back. He put it away, flashed a smile with big white teeth, but there was a subtle change in his attitude and it pleased her. It was no longer—at least for this moment—male to female, man to woman. He was Dave Jordan, whoever Dave Jordan was—but she was Juliette Gaza. He was a rook in an intricate chess game, she was a queen; he was another soldier in an army, she was a part of the military staff; he was a private in their complex corps, she a high officer. This was her job, her package, the campaign assigned her. She would give the orders and Jordan must obey and at this time, in this case, with this particular man, that total authority was so pleasant—damn you, Yagid—it was positively offensive.

"Just how much do you know about Konrad Kassel, Mr. Jordan?"

"Kassel?"

"Mannheim. His background, past history."

"I'm rather expert in his present history, Miss Gaza."

She couldn't resist. He was in line.

"People I like call me Julie."

"His past, Miss Gaza, isn't—wasn't—my business. But present—I think I've dredged up a hunk of information that's—to say the least—startling."

"One step at a time, Dave." She pointed at the sheaf of papers on the table. "I suggest you acquaint yourself with the material there."

"Yes, Miss Gaza." And the flash of his smile again. "May I?"

But he did not wait for consent from the commanding officer. He removed his jacket, hung it over the back of a chair. The pink shirt had short sleeves. His arms were long, powerful, muscular, and there was a good smell from him, a sweet masculine smell. Before he sat down he adjusted the pistol holster attached to his belt. Then he took up the papers and studied them while Juliette Gaza, covertly, studied him.

Obviously, a competent man. Loose and easy and outgoing, with a male-animal boldness just a shade away from male-animal arrogance, and so damned handsome, and he knew it. So, Miss Gaza, what complaint? If he didn't overstep in the business aspects, knew his place, knew who was boss—what complaint? Anna Stryker was immobilized and until there was word from Anna Stryker—and depending upon what that word was—there was time. And during that time there was time for yielding to personal pleasures. Why not? What complaint, Miss Gaza?

She crossed her knees and watched her man.

℞ Five

HE finished reading. He put the papers together neatly, laid them aside. He looked at her legs, then looked at her, smiled. He took a pipe and a pouch from a pocket of his jacket, filled the pipe, lit it.

"So?" he said.

18

"By the way," she said, "what are you supposed to do?"

"Do?" Dark eyebrows contracted in a squint.

"In Buenos Aires, here in New York, what's supposed to be your work, what do you do? How do they say it here in America? What's your racket?"

"I'm a writer, free-lance writer—with a small income from a small trust estate. Free-lance writer." He laughed. "For the male, that covers a multitude of sins. You can get up at noon, you can wander around days, you can stay up nights. Like for the female, free-lance model." He laughed again. "The finest prostitutes I've ever known, the most expensive of call girls—they all lump up under the same umbrella—free-lance models."

"Do you know many prostitutes?"

"Only professionally. No!" His laugh was full, melodious, boyish. "I mean that in reverse. *My* profession—well, alleged profession. A writer investigates all things, all people. As a matter of fact I do try to do some writing."

"Very interesting." She stood up, gestured toward the papers. "What do you think?"

He shrugged. "That's big stuff. I'm little stuff. The big stuff's none of my business."

"Nor mine for that matter, nor Shinbet's. His connection with the National Socialist League of Argentina; his close connection with the notorious *Blau Gruppe;* his imminent return to Germany as some kind of exiled national hero; their plans gradually to prime him as their candidate for Chancellor—none of our business. He has his rights and we have no right to interfere with his rights.

"But the past business of SS Colonel Konrad Kassel, Commander of Camp Number Six at Auschwitz—that *is* our business. The man who in two months funneled sixty thousand human beings to their deaths, a mass murderer—if he is—that damn well *is* our business. He escaped all penalty—some thought properly so, others did not—and that, a past problem of our people, has now become a present problem. Did you note the names of the concentration camp prisoners, Jews of Auschwitz, who testified in his defense? And they were subjected to severe cross-examination by the most imperative of interrogators who, however reluctantly, had to accede that the testimony was true. Unbelievable as it may sound, three

Jews scheduled for death in the ovens of Birkenau rescued their jailer, the commander of Camp Six, SS Colonel Konrad Kassel. Did you note their names?"

"Alfred Holzer, Jacob Stryker, Benjamin Jankowski."

"Jankowski and Stryker are dead. Holzer is still alive, hale and hearty, right here in New York, but right now that is not the point. We'll have an opportunity to talk with Holzer. The important thing is, Jacob Stryker had two children, two daughters, Anna Stryker and Gertrude Stryker, and four days ago, a person appeared before Gideon Rabin in the consulate here and that person mentioned the criminality of one Konrad Kassel—the first word in all these years even *hinting* at disingenuousness. And that person's name? Anna Stryker."

"What did she say?"

"Not enough. Rabin is diplomacy, not Shinbet. Diplomacy writes up the preliminaries, passes along the person to us. Not his job. Our job."

"You've examined her?"

"No."

"The hell."

"Please listen." And she swiftly outlined the Anna Stryker situation. "We'll talk with her as soon as they let us. If she says the kind of words we hope she does—we're ready. The jet waits at the airport, and my trunks are here. Would you come with me, please?"

She led him to the bedroom in which the trunks were.

"Try," she said. "Shove them around. I'm not yet unpacked."

Again his dark squint, querulous. He shrugged, pushed at the trunks. They were heavy.

"This one," she said. "Empty." She took keys from her handbag, unlocked the trunk, opened the thick metal hinge-clips, pulled open the top. "It's steel-lined, that's why it's so heavy. Get in," she said and at his askance look, smiled. "Just trying you for size," she said.

He climbed into the trunk, pulled up his knees, lowered his head, and she closed the cover.

"How's it feel?"

No answer.

"How's it feel?" More loudly.

The reply came as though from far away, muffled.

"All right."

"Comfortable?"

"Good enough."

She lifted up the trunk-lid and it remained open on its metal stays. "Those straps in there—with which I did *not* bind you— they'll hold him, keep him from being hurt no matter how the trunk is handled. And from where you are, from the inside with the light coming through, you can probably see the tiny, almost invisible vents—so the dear man won't suffocate."

"Yes, I see."

"Thank you, Dave."

She reached in to help him out, giving him leverage as the long legs deftly stepped over the side of the trunk, but he kept holding her hands, drawing her to him. His mouth came to hers but she moved her head aside. Instantly he released her.

"There won't be—there won't be any trouble at Customs." Her heart was pounding, she was having trouble with her breathing— the damn devil of a man. "Actually it's a government plane with full reciprocal clearance. Whether I take him or you take him— and it's quite possible Miss Stryker will also come—I don't anticipate any trouble whatever. Your passport? It's in order?"

"Of course."

"Rabin will provide the visa."

"Yes."

She stood for a moment at the window, looking out. "New York. I love this city."

"You've been here before?"

"Many times."

He sounded disappointed. "And I thought—well—I'd show you around a bit."

"I don't know it *that* well." She smiled, slyly. "Perhaps. Perhaps, if we have time." She came away from the window. "And now, Dave, your turn. I've given you all of my side, now yours. What about this startling information of yours? Oh. Would you like a drink?" She looked at her watch. 10:25. "Or is it too early for you?"

21

"Not too early for you?"

A brief laugh, very girlish. A flirtatious laugh, a female-to-male enticing chortle. Don't, Julie. Resist. Don't play his game with him. Not now. Not yet. "Like your free-lance writers, your free-lance models—I have no special hours. No, not too early for me." She went to a trunk, brought out a bottle. "Brandy. I always travel with brandy." A smile, simpering. Flirtatious, stupid. Stop it! "Sorry. I don't have proper glasses. We'll use tumblers from the bathroom. All right?"

"Sure."

"Not too early for you?"

"No."

She carried the bottle and the tumblers from the bathroom to the sitting room, deposited them on the table. He sat, crossed his legs, lit his pipe. She took up the bottle, began to pour. "Say when."

"When," he said. "Thank you, Miss—Julie."

She poured for herself, sipped. "Good." She sat. "So?"

"Konrad Mannheim, Importer. Mannheim Incorporated, Two-seventy-seven Park Avenue, New York, warehouse in Trenton, New Jersey. Konrad Mannheim, frequent visitor, supposedly business, to Buenos Aires, Argentina."

"Konrad Mannheim," she mimicked. "Home residence, Two-eighteen Central Park South." And sipped brandy.

"Konrad Mannheim, member of a fascist organization, the National Socialist League of Argentina, a pretty much secret group. I learned a lot about the League, and Mannheim's activities with the League, through this guy Harbin, Walter Harbin, who's been costing us three hundred bucks a week for a long time now."

"Yes I know. Just who is he, this Walter Harbin?"

"Quite the character. Thief, poet, adventurer, soldier of fortune, incurable romantic. Quite cultured. A linguist. A hell-raiser who grabs for money wherever the grabbing is good. Drifted down to Buenos Aires where he got himself in solid with the National Socialist League. Strictly for angles, not for politics. He's been our source, invaluable."

"A European? An American?"

"American as apple pie. Anyway, it was maybe a week ago that Harbin came up with a big one for me, my startling hunk of information." Jordan sucked on his pipe. "You've got to understand about that League down there; it's enormously rich, maybe fifty million bucks in its treasury, maybe more. And you've got to understand about Mannheim, a guy making a living in his own business but far from rich. And you've got to understand about a guy named Lubeck."

"Who?"

"Ludwig Lubeck."

"Who's Lubeck?"

"A German, a Bavarian, came to South America about twenty years ago with elderly parents, veteran Nazis who've long since passed on to their reward. Anyway, this Lubeck's been a fixture with the League for many years, risen all the way up to office of treasurer. A big, burly guy, heavily German, but an insignificant sort of guy, kind of hapless and insecure, and an absolute hero-worshipper of our suave Konrad Mannheim."

"By the way, have you ever met Mannheim?"

"Never. You?"

"No," she said. "Please go on."

"Well, as I said, it was maybe a week ago my friend Harbin —my friend that is on my payroll—came to me with the following information. Seems that Lubeck was pecking away at the League's treasury funds, peculating. And he had a large hunk of loot stashed away."

"What do you consider large, Mr. Jordan?"

"Are you ready, Miss Gaza?"

She smiled. "Ready."

"One million bucks in American money, cold cash. Large?"

"Large," she said. "And where was this—how did you say?—stashed?"

"Right here in America, in the States. Lubeck, during visits here, had brought it up."

She poured more brandy into their glasses. "And how did your friend Harbin know this, and why would he bring this information to you?"

Pipe in mouth, Jordan nodded approval. "You're a good advocate, Miss Gaza."

"People I like call me Julie," she said and sipped brandy. She

23

was listening with half an ear, relaxing, enjoying the company, enjoying the gossip. Anna Stryker was immobilized. There was time.

"Two good questions, Julie. And both have one answer. Mannheim."

Her glass slammed down to the table.

"Mannheim!" Now it was, whatever it was, pertinent.

He seemed pleased finally to have roused her.

"My friend Harbin, an experienced man and a devious man, had planted an electronic listening device in Lubeck's telephone. His job for me, at three hundred bucks a week, was Mannheim, and since in Buenos Aires the said Mr. Lubeck was Mannheim's closest crony, Harbin had this bug in Lubeck's phone. Anyway, he overheard a long conversation. Gist—Lubeck had the money in the States and Mannheim was to be his partner. Seems they had worked out this deal together with no skin off Mannheim's back—he was the silent partner. Sooner or later the embezzlement would be discovered with Lubeck, and Lubeck alone, the culprit. But by then Mannheim, scheduled in the near future to leave permanently for Germany, would take Lubeck with him and there secure him. A change of name, perhaps even a change of appearance, a small farm in a bucolic district, and Ludwig Lubeck would live happily ever after. When the bombshell would burst in Buenos Aires, Lubeck would be long gone, disappeared. And each of them—Lubeck and Mannheim—would be a half million dollars richer."

Silence now, a long silence. Jordan drew on his pipe with no response. It made a gurgling sound but produced no smoke. He cleared used tobacco from the bowl into an ashtray, refilled the pipe, tamped at the mouth of the bowl with his thumb.

"Dave."

Alertly. "Julie?"

"Is it possible that your Mr. Harbin was endeavoring to perpetuate his three hundred dollars a week?"

"Perpetuate?"

"Continuing to be useful—at three hundred per week—by inventing wild if interesting stories?"

"No."

"You think he was telling the truth?"

"I *know* he was telling the truth."

"He produced a tape of this alleged conversation?"

"No."

"Naïveté doesn't suit you, Mr. Jordan."

"Not naïve."

"Look. You called me a good advocate before, a compliment. Let me pursue that. Whatever the man told you, he *told* you. Hearsay, pure and simple. No proof, no corroboration. Dave, we're in the business. How in hell could you know this man wasn't fabricating?"

"I know. If you'll let me finish."

"Do. Please."

He sipped from his glass. The brandy had put a dull flush on his cheekbones. It enhanced his dark looks.

"Day before I received Yagid's cable, my friend Harbin asked me over to his apartment. A gorgeous place; leave it to Harbin. A penthouse apartment on the twenty-second floor of one of the best houses in Buenos Aires. We had a couple of convivial drinks, and then he propositioned me."

"Well now, proposition. That's much better than hearsay, Dave."

"He pressed his proposition with a bit of blackmail, but no matter. He told me Lubeck was coming up to the States, finally and permanently. Mannheim was my interest he said, but Lubeck was his interest, and if we, a couple of seasoned operators, pooled our interests, then he and I would divide that million between us rather than Mannheim and Lubeck."

"Interesting. How do they call it here?—moonlighting. Still working on your job, you get rich on the side."

He shook his head. "You're either corrupt or you're not corrupt, no two ways. You've got to look at your face every morning when you shave, and at night you want to sleep. There are those who can make it and those who can't. I can't, never could."

"You turned down the moonlight? A half million dollars?"

"But flatly—to my friend's astonishment."

"How flatly, Dave?"

"Flatly."

"*How* flatly?"

He struck a match to his pipe. He tilted his head, his strong jawline showing, puffed, blew a cone of smoke toward the ceiling. Then his head came level and his eyes met hers. With a strange impact. With force. Like fists.

"Unfortunately it was necessary. I killed him."

꧁ Six

THE sunlight through the windows was bright and warm, the odor of the pipe tobacco pleasant and comfortable. Blue smoke made slow, peaceful designs wafting upward. The dark, handsome man took the tumbler in a firm hand, sipped, set it down. He smiled but his eyes were sad.

"Have you ever killed, Miss Gaza? Do you know what it's like?"

She was silent. A corner of her mouth twitched. Then she said, "I've been a field agent for Shinbet for the past twelve years." And that remained her answer.

He nodded. With respect. He said in his deep calm voice, "It was necessary."

"What happened?"

"It was Harbin's idea that if we stayed close to Mannheim, we'd get very close to that money."

"Why not close to Lubeck?"

"That would be more difficult. Lubeck would be playing it cat and mouse. Lubeck had guilt. Not Mannheim. Mannheim, free and clear, would be in the open. Anyway it was Harbin's idea that Lubeck would be his man, Mannheim mine. Between us— with possibly the murder of both of them on our hands—there would be the pot of gold at the end of the rainbow."

"When is this Lubeck due in the States?"

"Today as a matter of fact."

She offered more brandy. He shook his head. She corked the bottle.

"And so you turned down his proposition."

"But flatly."

"But why *that* flatly?"

"I believe I—mentioned blackmail?"

"You did."

He reamed out his pipe, put it away.

"It seems my friend Harbin was doing investigation two ways —*for* me and *at* me. Now in retrospect there's no question he'd checked out my apartment while I was out of it, or even while I was in it, asleep. Quite a guy, my friend Harbin. Anyway he knew exactly who I was and what I was and whom I was working for, and that kind of knowledge in the possession of one like Harbin. . . ." He tapped his knees, stood up, paced. "It would have finished me with Shinbet, or else for the rest of my life I'd be working for Harbin. You know. An exposed agent is not an agent but a tool: to keep his job, he also has to work for the other guy. It's happened before; in our business we know it. Sometimes before you retire you can make a lot of money but you're a tool and, Christ, you have to live with yourself."

"What about his *own* risk? Exposing himself *to* you—as part of his exposure *of* you?"

"With a million bucks in the balance free and clear—a half million for each of us—he wasn't taking too much of a chance. He was offering me a fortune and putting on a little pressure to dissuade my reluctance. How could he lose? We—all of us— judge by our own standards. He was betting on a sure thing. There are no sure things. He gambled on a sure thing but he lost. I didn't win. Nobody won. I had no alternative."

"How?"

"I pretended to go along, but he was a dead man already. He outlined ideas, plans. But I wasn't listening. I was waiting, judging, measuring, thinking. Self-preservation. My own preservation, a great deal of the work of Shinbet. He had crept in where he didn't belong. He had trespassed, knowing the risk—and now he threatened. A million dollars, split two ways. Blackmail on a sure thing, but he lost. Nobody won. I set him up, and struck. A judo chop. With all my strength. To the nape. I broke his neck. Christ, you could hear the bones go."

"No. Bad." She spoke before she thought. Involuntary. Criti-

27

cism of technique, not morality. That was their business, esoteric, sometimes foul. The man had gambled, lost. A paid mercenary, he had turned on his donor. A traitor, he had met his penalty. To hell with this Harbin now dispatched to hell—what of over-all consequences? "Crude," she said. "Bad. Murder, pure, and murder never leaves the murderer alone. For the rest of your life—you're a target. If they seek you, they'll be seeking beyond you, and beyond you—Shinbet. Bad, Mr. Jordan. In our business, crude is bad. Alive he would have impaired your usefulness, but so does he dead."

"I'm sorry you consider me that stupid. Of course you don't know me."

"What's to know? Murder. You set him up, you broke his neck. Murder, open. What's to know?"

"No murder at all—that's what's to know." He tapped his pistol holster. "I could have shot him. I didn't. Can you read Spanish?"

"A little."

He took his jacket from the chair, slipped into it, withdrew his wallet and from that extracted a short newspaper clipping. "From the evening paper of the day he died. Nine lines. Facts. Unimportant news. Sort of obituary. Wish me to read and translate?"

"Nine lines? I should be able to handle it." She took the clipping and read, slowly, about Walter Harbin, age forty-one, a United States citizen living in Buenos Aires, who was dead by suicide. No relatives. The body was unclaimed.

"Suicide?" she said, but in a mollified tone. She returned the clipping. "How do you commit suicide by breaking your neck? The nape? The back of your neck?"

"It didn't show, Miss Gaza."

"Tell me, please."

He paced without footfalls on the thick carpeting and his voice was soft. "He was dead—of necessity. Certainly it couldn't be murder and certainly the broken neck would have to fit." He sighed, paced, chin down, his hands clasped behind him. "On his own typewriter I typed a simple suicide note and left it in the typewriter—'There comes a time for all of us, each for his own reasons. For me my time has come. May the Lord forgive me.' Nothing elaborate, that was it." He sighed again, unclasped his hands, walked the carpet. "Penthouse apartment, Miss Gaza. Twenty-second floor, a corner apartment, some of the windows to the rear." Now he spoke quickly. "The note in the typewriter, I was ready. I raised a rear window, carried him to it, slid him out head first, held him by the ankles, let him drop. All of the top of him had to be smashed. Gory, horrible, but no pain—please remember he was already dead. Then, quite simply, I left. My place was far away, all the way across town. I went home. And next day, the cablegram—Yagid's cable."

She was silent and he stood stock-still in the silence. Strong. A strong man. She considered more brandy but as she bent toward the bottle he put up his hand. "No," he said and then the hand pointed a finger at the papers on the table. "So," he said, "when we take him—if and when we take him—there might be a bonus, a half million dollars worth of bonus."

"We're not interested in bonuses. We're interested in him. *If* we're interested in him. Depends on what we hear from Anna Stryker."

"A man died. Would you refuse the bonus?"

"Who said refuse?" Her laugh was mirthless. "That's what bonus means—bonus, something additional." She stood up. "Would you like to meet him?"

"Whom?"

"Mannheim, who else?"

"When?"

"Now. He travels to Germany often, on business, stays long; he's well known there. One of the places he visits, often, is an export house, Stuttgart Novelties, in West Germany that does good business with Mannheim Incorporated in America. He has met most of the executives of Stuttgart Novelties and he has heard of its star salesman—rather, saleswoman—the international Miss Gina Juliette, but he has never met her. Now he will meet her."

"You?"

"Stuttgart Novelties is one of our cover operations and I"—she made a little bow—"am Gina Juliette, fairly reeking with credentials. And you? You'll be who you are, Dave Jordan, a writer, and not quite who you are—a close friend of Miss Juliette, her boyfriend—*ami*—here in New York. A good idea, don't you think, to get to know Konrad Mannheim, perhaps even socially? It will help, if and when. . . ." She looked at her watch. "Yes?"

"Yes," he said, and grinned. "Two-seventy-seven Park, it's at Forty-eighth Street. We're at Park and Fifty-ninth. It's a few minutes."

"Yes," she said.

277 Park Avenue was another of the tall, stark, all-glass, all-American office buildings, and Mannheim Incorporated was a modest suite on the fourteenth floor with a pert young receptionist who quickly put through the callers to Kurt Goritz, Mr. Mannheim's first assistant.

"Ah, yes, Miss Juliette, I'm so terriby sorry," said Goritz in a neat wood-paneled office. He was small, bald, obsequious, obviously impressed. "Gina Juliette—anything, anything at all I can do for you. Such a surprise, and Mr. Mannheim—he'll be so terribly disappointed. He's away."

"Away? Where?"

The bald man lifted his hands. "Who knows, with Mr. Mannheim? A genius in his own right, Mr. Mannheim. A buying trip. He pokes into all corners of the world." Yellow teeth erupted in a sad smile. "Who ever knows with Mr. Mannheim?"

"Doesn't he contact the office?"

"Rarely, when he's off on one of his buying trips."

"Can't you reach him?"

The yellow smile, helpless. "I wish I could say I could."

"But it's important, Mr. Goritz."

"It's not the first time I've heard that, Miss Juliette. I don't have to dissemble with you, do I? I'm supposed to be in charge when he's gone—and I am in charge when he's gone—but who, really, am I? I'm nobody, that's who I am; I don't have to dissemble with you, Miss Juliette, do I? It's essentially a one-man operation here and Mr. Mannheim is that one man. I'm so terribly sorry; he'll be so terribly disappointed."

"How long?"

"Pardon, Miss Juliette?"

"How long has he been gone?"

"Two weeks."

"And when will he return?"

The sad yellow smile. "He said six weeks—but who knows with Mr. Mannheim."

"Thank you, Mr. Goritz."

"I'm so sorry, Miss Juliette."

Downstairs she said, "I don't believe him."

"Why?" Jordon asked. "Why would this guy want to lie to the star saleslady of Stuttgart Novelties?"

"Not actually lying, simply following instructions is what I mean. A business man doesn't go off on a buying trip without being in touch with his office. Goritz told us what Mannheim told him to tell."

"Which means Mannheim, for some reason, is ducking, hiding out."

"Perhaps it has something to do with that Lubeck affair."

"For a half million bucks, tax free—can you blame him?"

"Wherever he is, we've got to know. If the word from Anna Stryker is not the word we hope—then none of it is any of our business, he goes his way as he wishes. But if her word makes him prey—then we must have a line on him, we *must* know where to pick him up."

"Yes," Jordan said mildly. "But how?"

"There are specialists for every purpose, there are specialists for tracing a man, finding a man. The specialist we choose must be absolutely discreet." She laughed. Grimly. "Age of specialization. You're a specialist, I'm a specialist. We're neither of us I don't think particularly brilliant, but in our specialty we *are* brilliant. And there are other brilliant specialists in *their* fields. What time is it?"

He looked at his wrist. "Eleven-thirty."

"We'll go to Rabin. He'll give us a good man, the best. I'll handle that end. You—you'll take care of Holzer. We'll have Rabin contact him. You'll bring Holzer to me at the hotel"—she thought for a moment—"at two-thirty. By two-thirty I should be finished with whoever turns out to be our specialist. Am I—how do you Americans say it?—am I on the beam, Dave?"

"Right on the nose."

"What?" she said.

"On the beam," he said. "And may I add . . .?"

31

"Another American colloquialism?"

"No, " he said. "Just—you're very beautiful."

He hailed a taxi. She gave the driver the address of the consulate on East 70th Street.

༄ Seven

McGREGOR momentarily held away Shakespeare's *Othello* and looked at his belly in the bathtub and was pleased with what he saw—flatness shimmering in the early morning sunshine; that is, early morning for McGregor. The clock had rung at eleven and he had shut it off, yawned, stretched, dozed, then had opened his eyes, contemplating the new day, and a fine day it was to be. To begin with, it was target-day. Today ended a long and strenuous diet.

When he had looked again at the clock, fifteen minutes had sped by. Morning for McGregor at 11:15—why not? Depends upon when you go to sleep, he thought. He had gone to sleep at 4 A.M. after a lovely, languorous evening with Tillie Ulrich. Ah, my Tillie, he thought, wondrous Tillie, always surprising. He got out of bed and did fifty push-ups with consummate ease, then opened a window, blithely tossed off an intricate series of yoga exercises, and then admired himself in front of a tall mirror: svelte McGregor. And laughed. It works, he thought, if you work at it. Ladies and gentlemen of the world, if you wish to lose weight it is simple: don't eat so much. That's the whole story: don't eat so much. Forget the steak-and-coconut-juice diets; forget skim milk and bananas and vitamin pills; forget the no-carbohydrates bull and baloney; forget the ten-day fasts; forget the new-breed doctors who furnish you with lists of no-fat foods and the pills every two weeks at twenty bucks a crack, the amphetamines that make you fly in the company of company at parties but make you sullen and reluctant at home in bed with your mate—forget! Eat what you always ate but half as much or, if necessary, a quarter as much, and you'll be as delightfully slender as I, me, McGregor laughing at himself in the mirror.

He had a program. Because he was a pig. Pig, he thought, the euphemism is gourmet. Yes I am the hell a gourmet, and damn happy about it, he thought, but as you get old you have got to watch out for the gourmet-frankenstein you have built inside of you. Old? Would Tillie, after last night, say I am old? And the gleeful laugh at the slim reflection in the mirror—slim for him— froze to a scowl. Yessir, damn, I *am* old. Feel like a boy, but the calendar says. I've got the muscles, the testicles, the whole damn bravura, but the calendar says. When you're pushing fifty, mister, the calendar says you are old no matter how you feel and so you have to watch out for the cholesterol and the rest of that crap and arrange for yourself a program and I have arranged. When you have a frame that measures all the way up to six-foot-three and you like to eat, you balloon. And when you *really* balloon, mister, you become a bawcock with an avoirdupois of two-fifty which, your doctor tells you, is, for you, dangerous. Optimum for you: two-ten. And so you have arranged for you a program: three months of rigor and six months of living the way you like to live. The three months of eating half of what you normally eat—or down to a quarter depending upon the bathroom scale—thins you to what the medic considers optimum, and then the next six months of living like a human being slowly puts it on again. The doc also hollers about cigarettes but too late. Cigarettes, you're an addict. They've got you coming and going: the simple pleasant pleasures are somehow the quick conduits to death, a hell of a lousy paradox when you put your mind to it. How far along do you go with the learned doctors who themselves, when you meter the professions, die fairly young? Is the only purpose of life to live a long life? The hell with it.

McGregor lit a cigarette and thought about breakfast and dismissed the thought. Breakfast today would be brunch because dinner today would be the most lavish of the year, and he went to the bathroom and stood on the scale and was proud of the corroboration: he had knocked optimum for a loop. Skinny McGregor weighed in at 202 and, looking down, no pot-belly obscured his view of the rest of him. He trotted to the kitchen, squeezed juice, made coffee, and then somewhat assuaged picked up a copy of *Othello,* drew a tub and immersed himself in hot water and Shakespeare.

When the phone rang, the wall-clock in the bathroom expressed ten minutes to noon. McGregor reached for the handset thinking, as he always thought when talking from the bath, of electrocution by the grace of A.T.&T. It was Tillie Ulrich.

"Hi, beloved," he said.

"How are you, Maestro?" Sultry the voice, even in the forenoon.

"Fit—as R. L. Stevenson once put it—and taut as a fiddle."

"What was *that?* I heard a splash."

"*Othello* fell into the tub. Pardon a moment; I'm rescuing." A pause. "All right, I'm back."

"Soaking, Mr. McGregor?"

"Lolling, Miss Ulrich."

"Anticipating?"

"Oh but yes. And remember what I told you last night. Eat just once—about this time would be the right time—and then don't dare eat again until we're all together."

"Right, Mr. Maestro. See you at four."

"Four o'clock, Miss Ulrich. Until then. . . ."

"Bye, love."

"Bye."

He hung up, patted and placed away the wet *Othello.* He stretched out in the warmth, but no ordinary tub was long enough for him. He rested his neck on one end of the porcelain, his heels up on the other end; in between he laced his fingers over what had once been his paunch and considered the delights of reestablishing it. Today signaled a marvelous beginning. Today was the dinner of the Wine and Food Society.

Once a year the Wine and Food Society of New York, of which McGregor was a vice president and director, gave a dinner as host to another gourmet society—this year for the Confrerie des Chevaliers du Tastevin. Last year the big dinner had been at Le Pavillon; this year the Society had selected—a fine and merited

34

honor for Tillie—the restaurant she owned, Café Ulrich, which for this one day would be closed to the public.

They would gather at four o'clock—people flying in from all over the world—for greeting, meeting, talk, and camaraderie over hors d'oeuvre and aperitif; the dinner did not commence until seven.

McGregor, stirring in his steaming bath, remembered last year's dinner, remembered it all, exactly, precisely—the people, what they looked like, where they were seated, what they were wearing, and his mind drifted to the business of memory: blessing or curse? He was blessed—or cursed—with total recall. A photographic memory, the Inspector, they used to say of McGregor when he was with Homicide in the New York City Police Department. Blessing or curse? And McGregor remembered what others had said. Disraeli: "A good memory is often as ready a friend as a sharp wit." And Mr. Shakespeare: "Memory, the warder of the brain." And Cicero: "Memory is the treasury of all things and their guardian." But Montaigne tartly had said—and McGregor laughed in his bath, recollecting—"Experience teaches that a good memory is usually joined to a weak judgment." But it had been Cicero, later quoted by the tart Montaigne, who had expressed the curse: "Forgetfulness, rather; for I remember even those things which I would not, and cannot forget what I would."

The ring of the phone roused him from revery, and he reached for it hastily. Tillie again, lovely Tillie, poor Tillie today: nervous, excited, on mettle to the most famous of experts. But it was not Tillie.

"Mr. McGregor?" A lady. A crisp British voice.

"This is he."

"May I see you, sir?"

Chuckle. "If you did at this moment I imagine you'd be rather shocked."

"Beg pardon?"

"No matter. What is it, ma'am?"

"I should like to see you. On business."

"When?"

"Right away, if possible."

"Well . . ." McGregor said.

"Urgent, Mr. McGregor. It's most important."

"Well . . ." McGregor said and looked up at the clock. "Would you like to have lunch with me?"

"Lunch?"

"Lunch."

"Where?"

"Here."

"But isn't this your office?"

"Office and home, one and the same. My office is my home and vice versa."

"Oh." And during the moment of silence he could feel, somehow, her smile through the wires of A.T.&T. "Yes," she said. "Thank you for the invitation."

"It's Seventy-fifth and Central Park West. The San Remo. Fifteenth floor."

"Yes, I know."

He looked again at the clock. "Twelve-thirty?"

"Excellent," she said.

And hung up before he hung up.

℞ Eight

SHE started, startled, when he opened the door. She covered by coughing and covered that with stammered apologies for the paroxysm. She had expected an old man. A retired inspector of Police, Rabin had told her, now a private detective, as a sort of avocation. Rich in his own right, Rabin had told her, by reason of judicious investments through a long career and further supported by a sturdy pension from the Police Department, he was nevertheless (perhaps because he did not need the money) the most expensive private detective in the City of New York. A bachelor, a dilettante, rather an eccentric, but absolutely brilliant. She had expected a wizened, crotchety, elderly gentleman. . . .

He was not old, not elderly. He was very tall, vibrant, straight as a tree, exceedingly handsome, a woman's man, a man for a woman, and she of all people, she could appreciate that. He had frosty white hair but jet-black eyebrows. His face, with a stubborn jutted chin, was lean, pink, strong-boned, and he had the eyes of an eagle but blue. His eyes were the barrier, cold-blue, and even now smiling: remote, somehow disdainful, piercing.

He took her out of the doorway and into an elegant apartment.

"Beautiful," she said.

"Pardon?" A deep male rumble, from the chest.

"Your place here. Lovely."

"Thank you." No names, not once had he asked her name.

He led her to a dining room, to a table covered with white linen and gleaming silver. "Please," he said and took the manila envelope from her and her handbag and placed them on a side-table. "Please," he said and held a chair for her. "Thank you," she said and sat. "In a moment," he said and went out and came back with a tray and served. Shrimp cocktail, the huge shrimps on a bed of green lettuce and diced celery, the bowl of the shrimps set within a wider bowl of chopped ice. Hot biscuits within a nest of cloth in a wicker basket. Lumped, golden, tub-butter. A platter of Melba toast. And the most delicious cocktail sauce she had ever tasted.

"This sauce," she said. "Absolutely exquisite."

"Shrimp sauce is shrimp sauce," he said. "Ketchup, horse-radish, Worcestershire sauce, and vinegar in proper proportion. The secret of my sauce—and I make no secret of my secrets—is to add a dash of Angostura bitters, a dash of *fines herbes,* a touch of sherry and a touch of port. Lemon, of course."

"Mr. McGregor."

"Ma'am?"

"Why I'm here. My husband. Ex-husband. Mr. Konrad Mann-heim."

"Not now, please, Mrs. Mannheim. First we eat. Then business."

"Not Mrs. Mannheim. I use my maiden name. Gaza. Juliette Gaza."

"Lovely; a lilting name. After lunch, Miss Gaza?"

"But Americans—don't they always talk business during lunch?"

"Some Americans. Not this American."

An eccentric, Rabin had said.

"As you wish, Mr. McGregor."

After the shrimp he went away for a time and then came back with fluffy omelets and steaming coffee, and she was enjoying her best lunch in years.

"The coffee. . . ."

"Half Mocha, half Columbia. I get them in the green bean, roast them here, grind fresh before each brewing."

"The best I've ever had."

"Thank you, Miss Gaza."

"And another question. Please don't think me impertinent."

She was interested in food, she talked food: already he liked her.

"Not at all," he said.

"This delicious omelet. I know about omelets—there are people who have the gift and those who don't, and you certainly do. But the color—the perfectly beautiful golden color?"

"Saffron," he said. "Somehow not greatly popular in this country. A judicious sprinkle of saffron. Gives color, but also subtly adds flavor."

And then as subtle as saffron—she was aware and admired—he turned the conversation, probing for a subject that would interest her, and they settled into a fine talk about ladies' clothes, *haute couture* and international fashion. Quite a man, this Mc-Gregor. And just as subtly, the luncheon finished, he brought her back to business. "Forgive me," he said, "I've been selfish. I enjoy food but even more I enjoy the presence of a beautiful woman. I hope I haven't imposed on you, your time."

"Not at all, and I thank you. For the compliment, for a wonderful lunch."

He smiled, lit a cigarette. "And so?"

"Konrad Mannheim, my ex-husband."

"What brought you to me, Miss Gaza?"

"I was recommended."

"By whom?"

"I—I'd rather not say."

"All right." He nodded. "As you wish."

"You see—alimony. It came, always promptly, regularly. I've been living in England. He would send it directly—every week. Suddenly it stopped. Three weeks ago. It never happened before."

"How long are you divorced?"

"Five years. Never happened before. And—well—he's not in his office, hasn't been for the past two weeks. I—I'm worried."

"Office? Where?"

"Here in New York."

"And you've been living in England?"

"Yes."

"When did you come over?"

"Today."

"Because of—this irregularity in alimony?"

"He seems to have disappeared."

"Is that why you came over, Miss Gaza?"

She hesitated. "Frankly, no. I—I came over to visit with my fiancé. An arrangement before, we arranged it, my fiancé and I, before."

"Fiancé?"

"A Mr. Dave Jordan here in the city. Not the point, Mr. McGregor. The point—I'm worried about Mr. Mannheim."

"You're on good terms with him?"

"Not good, not bad. Five years, a long time." She sipped cold coffee. "This must be confidential, Mr. McGregor. If and when you discover him for me, he mustn't know I engaged a private detective."

"Of course not."

"All I want to know—if he's all right and alive and where he is."

McGregor stubbed out his cigarette, lit another. His beautiful prospective client was a liar. What she was lying about—not his business. When an ex-husband is delinquent in alimony, the ex-wife consults her lawyer, not a strange private detective—nor would she make a secret to the private detective as to who recommended her. Not on particularly good terms with the ex-husband, the ex-wife would not be particularly interested in his well-being except for the matter of alimony—and that would be lawyer-business, not detective-business. Nor would an ex-wife be interested in the whereabouts of an ex-husband, especially not an ex-wife with a fiancé (fiancé meaning, in this loose, hip, latter-half twentieth century—sexual lover).

"You want me to find him for you. Is that it, Miss Gaza?"

"Yes," she said and sounded relieved. "I want to see him, talk to him."

"About the break in the alimony payments?"

"I have other—personal reasons."

"All right," he said. "Tell me a bit about Mr. Mannheim. What's his business?"

"He's an importer. Buys from foreign countries, sells here."

"The address of his office?"

"Two-seventy-seven Park Avenue—Mannheim Incorporated."

"Home address?"

"Two-eighteen Central Park South. Apartment 4A."

"And now description." The cold blue eyes were inscrutable. "How good are you at description, Miss Gaza?"

"No need," she said. She stood up, held herself erect, aware of her figure, aware of its impression on him. A charming, interesting man. Were she not here in this country strictly for business, were she here for a long stay—this would be a man she would want to cultivate. Dave Jordan? Another matter. Dave Jordan inspired the animal juices. Dave Jordan would be quick fun and as quickly forgotten. She crossed to the side table and came back with her pocketbook and the manila envelope, and from the envelope drew out two photographs of Konrad Mannheim and handed them across. McGregor studied the pictures, one a head-shot, one a full-shot, and returned them.

"Thank you."

"You may keep them, if you wish."

"Not necessary." His grin was amiable. "I am blessed—cursed? —with a retentive memory. Once I see a face, I never forget it. Remembrance. Total recall, photographic memory—curse or blessing, Miss Gaza?"

"A thorny question, Mr. McGregor." Her eyes narrowed, she spoke softly: " '*Les souvenirs embellissent la vie, l'oubli seul la rend possible*—remembrances embellish life but forgetfulness alone makes it possible.' "

"Beautiful." He applauded. "Damn true. Who said it?"

"I don't know. When I was a child, my father quoted it to me, and I've never forgotten it."

"Miss Gaza, you've hired yourself a detective."

"The fee, Mr. McGregor?" The brown eyes opened, smiling.

"Also a thorny question, and sometimes a sensitive one. Are you sensitive, Miss Gaza?"

"I think I am—but there are many who disagree. There are areas where one is sensitive, and areas where one is not."

"The going price for this kind of deal—a trace-job we call it— is one hundred dollars a day plus expenses. I charge double the going price."

"Would you accept a flat-fee arrangement?"

"Like how?" he said.

"I am—how best can I say it?—in a hurry. I don't expect to be here long—perhaps a week." She opened her handbag, put money on the table. "Time is of the essence. Here is two thousand dollars as a retaining fee. If you turn him up for me—and the sooner the better—an additional three thousand dollars."

He did not look at the money.

"Deal," he said. "But with a proviso."

"What?"

"From now until four o'clock, I'm at your service. From four o'clock until tomorrow morning, I'm engaged. After that, I'm *completely* at your service. But I work in my own way, in my own manner—without interference."

"Deal," she said.

He lit a new cigarette from the tip of the old cigarette.

"Bluntly now, Miss Gaza. All you want is to get hold of the guy. Correct?"

"Bluntly, yes."

"And where can I reach you?"

"The Delmonico Hotel. Suite Fourteen Hundred."

"And now just this, if you please, about your Mr. Mannheim.

Any reason—that you might know—about any possible jeopardy? Has he—that you might know—involvements? Personal? Business? Matters of the heart? Anything?"

She sat back, silent.

Then she said, "My ex-husband is a German."

"So? The lady to whom I'm engaged"—and he offered the amiable grin again—"unofficially engaged, is a German. So?"

"No, not ethnically, I'm talking politically. Mr. Mannheim is in Germany often, very often, and he's a member of right wing groups there, radical right-wingers, extremists. Yes, very possibly he *has* enemies, political enemies."

"Thank you. Anything else that might help?"

Silence. Then—"No, nothing I can think of."

He stood up. "I propose more coffee. Fresh coffee?"

" 'Candy is dandy, but liquor is quicker.' Whose is that?"

"Ogden Nash."

"Well, your coffee beats them both. You've seduced me, Mr. McGregor, but please, I must be out of here by two o'clock."

"We'll manage," he said.

℘ Nine

HOLZER worked for Harry Winston, Inc. Harry Winston, Inc., was one of the most famous jewelry houses in the world and Alfred Holzer was one of the most famous diamond experts in the world. When it came to diamond cutting—the delicate, painstaking, hazardous splitting of huge precious stones (bad balance, bad judgment, one bad stroke could mean the loss of hundreds of thousands of dollars)—Alfred Holzer had no peer. Sometimes as a courtesy to another jewelry house—on request and if the job was big enough—they would loan him out. *"Noblesse oblige,"* said Max Simon, the foreman of the shop. "There is only one Alfred Holzer."

When the phone rang a few minutes before the noontime lunchbreak, Simon was watching the old man seated at a counter, jeweler's loupe protruding from the socket of his right eye, deftly sorting small diamonds into three separate piles on black velvet cloths. What a man, Simon thought. Like another breed, these old boys. Seventy-four years old, rough and hearty, never a complaint, twenty-twenty vision, and hands as steady as precision instruments. The phone rang and Simon took it.

"Yes?"

"Is Mr. Holzer there?"

"He's busy right now. Who's calling?"

"Tell him Gideon Rabin. He'll know."

"Busy right now. You want to call back or hang?"

"I'll hang on."

"Right." Simon put down the receiver, went to Holzer. "For you. A Mr. Rabin."

"Tell him I'll ring him back. A few minutes."

"He said he'll hold."

"Okay."

When he was finished, the tall gaunt old man uncoiled from his seat and laid away the loupe. He pointed at the piles of stones. "These are excellent, these good, those fair. That's it."

"Right," said Simon.

The old man took up the stump of a black, bitten cigar and went to the phone. "Yes, Mr. Rabin?"

"Holzer?"

"Yes, Mr. Rabin."

"There's a man wants to talk to you. Man and lady, matter of fact. Important."

"Man and lady—what about?"

"The old, old matter."

"Oh." He sighed. It never ends, does it? He put the stub of the unlit cigar in a corner of his mouth, clenched it in firm teeth. I am seventy-four and every one in there is my own, never lost a tooth in my life. There are people like that. I'm a lucky old man. Lucky? "When?" he said.

"The man," Rabin said. "Name's Dave Jordan. He'll pick you

up at two. Where would you like? At your place? Or at home?"

"For how long?"

"I'd say. . . ." A pause. "A couple of hours, maybe."

"Just a minute." Holzer put his hand over the mouthpiece. "Max," he called. "This afternoon. I—I need a few hours."

"Sure. Something? The family?"

"Not the family."

"Thank God. A few hours when?"

"I have got to meet a man at two o'clock, then a few hours."

"Look, it's lunchtime already," Simon said. Steady as a rock, Holzer rarely asked a favor. "If at two o'clock you need a few hours and now already it's lunchtime—forget it, we can live without you here." Simon laughed. "Starting now, you're off. See you tomorrow."

"Thank you, Max."

"Don't mention it."

Holzer removed his hand from the mouthpiece. "Two o'clock I'll be home, Mr. Rabin."

"Good. He'll pick you up there. Dave Jordan."

"You know the address?"

"Yes. And—I realize the inconvenience, sir, and I do thank you. I knew I could depend on your cooperation. Thank you, Mr. Holzer."

"Don't mention it, Mr. Rabin."

He took a taxi home. He always used taxis. Thank God I can afford, he thought. I make a good living and taxis are especially for us, the old ones. He gave the driver the address—1040 Fifth Avenue—a fine address, one of the finest in America. Hooray, America. I love you very much.

Settled in the cab, he lit his cigar. A fine address but to me, meaningless. At my age, at my time, I can live anywhere. But to my son it is important; in a way it is a part of his profession. My son, this son, the last of my sons, is a famous surgeon, and a good address is part of the profession. Downstairs is the office. And high upstairs a triplex apartment is home.

My son, he thought, my youngest, the last of my children, the only one who survived. Three sons had died, and their mother, trying to escape in that time of madness so long ago. But this one, my youngest, then nineteen, he had accomplished the escape—aided and abetted by the Germans. We must not forget, we Jews. Because of the mad ones, the bigots, the Nazi-lovers, we cannot condemn an entire people.

Germans had saved his son. Germans of Dresden, the underground, had brought out Holzer's one remaining son, and Jankowski's wife, and Stryker's wife and infant daughter. The wives had died en route but Holzer's son and Stryker's infant had safely arrived to Australia where Stryker's wife's parents lived. And it had been the Germans of Dresden who had hidden and harbored Alfred Holzer, and Benjamin Jankowski, and Jacob Stryker, and Stryker's tiny, valiant, emaciated elder daughter who was all of eleven years old when the war ended. Germans. Not Nazis. Not Nazi-lovers. Germans who at the risk of life and finally at the cost of life had hidden and harbored these four Jews and when discovered, almost at war's end, had been summarily shot and the Jews transported to Auschwitz. No, my Jews, we must not condemn a whole people. Crimes must be individually sorted and judged. Condemnation by association—by groups, peoples, nationalities—is by far the greater crime. Of all peoples, certainly we Jews should know.

Alfred Holzer. Leathery, wrinkled, well-dressed, healthy. Smoking his cigar in the rear of the taxi. Stopping and starting in the New York traffic.

The son had not remained in Australia. By a devious route he had gone to Palestine. And there Alfred Holzer after release from Auschwitz, after testimony with Jankowski and Stryker at the Nuremberg trials—Stryker's elder daughter was by then with the grandparents in Australia—there in Palestine he had at last been reunited with the one remaining member of his family.

It had not been a difficult time. A diamond expert renowned in his field, he had resisted well-paying offers from jewelry houses in many parts of the world, and had settled into a business of his own in Haifa. He had withstood the labor pains of a new nation in birth and had emerged a well-to-do First Citizen. He had never remarried. He had supported his son in schools in Switzerland and America and the son had returned to Israel as a practicing surgeon, settling in Haifa.

In time the son had married and in ten years Alfred Holzer was the doting grandparent of six grandchildren. And then a new tragedy. Life takes its toll. The son's wife had been killed in an automobile accident. And six months later—life renews itself— Theresa O'Keefe, called Terry, had come on vacation from America to Haifa and his son and Theresa had joined in love.

She was a school teacher from the United States on a sabbatical in Israel. The son and the school teacher plotted marriage but on difficult terms for both (and also for Alfred Holzer). The son insisted that Terry give up her career, to which she was devoted, but in turn Terry insisted that if they marry they move to America. And so it had happened, and Alfred Holzer, then already an old man, had emigrated with his family: his son, his new daughter-in-law, his lovely grandchildren. Five years now. Time flies. There were two new little ones in the house, two new grandchildren, and the son was an American citizen. Not Alfred Holzer. He clung to his Israeli citizenship. An old man. An old man does not give up the old country.

He smoked his cigar. He visited, often, at the consulate with Mr. Rabin, talking about old-country matters, and had visited at Rabin's home, and Mr. and Mrs. Rabin had visited at his home. A fine, good man, Mr. Rabin.

Alfred Holzer raised a hand to his cheek and held it there as though he had a toothache. He suddenly remembered asking Rabin over the phone if he knew his address. Ach, he thought, don't tell me I'm really getting old.

"Ten-forty Fifth," the driver said.

"Fine, fine," Holzer said.

Terry looked concerned when he came in.

"What's the matter, Gramps?"

Gramps. He loved it. In America his new name. They all called him Gramps, the kids, even his son.

"Nothing, nothing the matter. Don't look so scared. I have to see a man about a . . . who knows what? So I figured I would have lunch home. He's coming here, the man."

"When?"

"Two o'clock."

"Oh then, lots of time."

"The kids? It's so quiet."

"Rita's got the little ones out in the park. The big ones—school. Look, Gramps. You'll have lunch with me. I just prepared it. There's enough for two."

"Your lunch," he said. "How's the boss?"

"At the hospital. Won't be home until three. So? Lunch with your *shiksa* daughter-in-law?"

"Your lunch."

"Tomato juice. Cottage cheese salad. Black coffee."

"That's what I mean. Me, I don't have to worry about my shape. Your shape? I couldn't wish better on my own son. No. Thanks for the cottage cheese. I was figuring on bacon, you should pardon the expression, and eggs. Sunnyside."

"We've got a slab of wild Irish bacon. Imported. Rita's father sent it over. Direct from Dublin."

"Personally—*you* should know—I'm a Canadian bacon man. Don't bother about Gramps. I'll fix it up myself."

"Not on your life. Canadian bacon and eggs, sunnyside up, country-style. Rye bread toast, well-buttered. Coffee, heavy cream on the side. Do I know what you like?"

"Who said Canadian?"

"Didn't you just say?"

"I am curious about Rita's father direct from Dublin. Happens Irish bacon I adore, sliced thin. Canadian is Canadian but wild Irish direct from Dublin, why not?"

"Gramps, you're a card. Sit down, I'll whip it up. My pleasure, an unexpected pleasure."

"Thank you. I'll go wash my hands."

At one o'clock the phone call was for Holzer. From Rabin.

"Mr. Holzer, I couldn't talk too well before."

"Pardon, Mr. Rabin?"

"The man, the lady—they were present when I called. I was —er—restricted. You know?"

"Sure. Sure, Mr. Rabin."

"Shinbet people."

"Yeah, who else? What else?"

"What *else?*"

"No, no, I mean who-else-what-else? The old matter; who else?"

"There seem to have been some developments."

47

"Yes, yes, always developments."

"I know, Mr. Holzer. Cruel. But they seem to think it necessary. Like ripping open old wounds. Believe me, I hate it."

"What . . . necessary? What can I tell them that I have not said before? It is in the trial record, a public record—me, Stryker, Jankowski."

"They're dead. You're alive."

"Does that change the public record?"

"They're young people, new people; they never heard. Of course they've read the record, but they never heard. You're the last. You must try to understand."

"Yes, I understand."

"I hate it."

"I understand."

"He will come at two o'clock—Mr. Jordan. And he will take you."

"Where?"

"The lady's at the Delmonico, the Delmonico Hotel. It is there they will talk to you. The appointment, two-thirty. I felt—I feel— I wanted you to know. I mean—the sequence. You know?"

"Yes. Thank you."

"You're very kind, Mr. Holzer."

"Me? Why? Why . . . I am kind?"

"Alfred, this is Rabin. Don't be brave with *me*."

"Necessary. If necessary—necessary. You just said it, just before. I am the one. Alive."

Silence on the other side.

"Mr. Rabin . . .?"

"Holzer, I—personally—I thank you."

"Don't mention it, Mr. Rabin."

"Two o'clock," Holzer said to his daughter-in-law. "At two o'clock he will come, a man for me, a Dave Jordan. You will kindly show him up to me, please?"

"I will kindly show him up to you please."

"Thank you."

"Don't mention." She grinned. "You'll take a nap in the meantime, as long as you're home?"

"No nap. But coffee, I would like to take."

"You bet. Go and relax. I'll bring it up."

"If you don't mind, I'll bring it myself."

"Naturally. Gramps, I love you. If your son hadn't happened to get in the way, I'd have married you."

"So who said you would be doing so bad?"

She laughed. "Who said bad?"

"Married, maybe no. At my age, too old, too wise. But if not for my son, a doll like you, a girlfriend. . . ."

"Me?" She giggled. *"My* type? Girlfriend?"

"You're different?"

"Gramps!" And went to make coffee, and called back: "Although I've been hearing rumors about you and a girlfriend. . . ."

"So? Why not?"

He took the pot of coffee upstairs to his apartment. Triplex, no less. Hooray, America. One apartment three floors, but in fact more than one apartment. Inside his son's apartment, he had his own apartment. Fancy in America, but like a *kibbutz* in the old country. Only here you pay rent. And proudly, adamantly, and despite his son's protestation, he paid his full, proportionate share of the rent—but expensive. Oh yessirree but expensive. But if you can afford, you afford. You pay your own way; till you die, if you can afford, you pay your own way.

He poured coffee into a cup, this time black, no sugar. He lit a fresh, new, long cigar, sat by the window, smoked, sipped coffee, and looked out on the sunshine dappling the green park, and remembered. He knew why they wanted to talk to him, the young ones, the new ones. Stryker was dead. Jankowski was dead. Alfred Holzer was alive and he could repeat the story of the son who had killed the father, the Nazi colonel who, crazed with shock and horror, had condemned and executed the Nazi general for the atrocities of genocide committed at Auschwitz.

There had been Holzer, Jankowski, Stryker, and Stryker's little girl, the wisp of a child eleven years old, captured in Dresden at war's end, the last of the prisoners brought to Auschwitz. And there at Camp No. 6 they had requested and been granted an audience with the commander of Camp No. 6, SS Colonei Konrad

49

Kassel. During the years of hiding, protected by Germans of Dresden, they had learned, they knew, what was to be their fate if captured—and they knew that the war was virtually over. And so as a committee they had pleaded for the Jews of Camp No. 6—not to be transferred to Birkenau, to be spared in these last days, to be permitted to live. The war was over; in a few days it would be all over. They knew: they were from the outside. They had asked mercy of the commander of Camp No. 6—not only for the Jews of Camp No. 6 but for all the rest of the Jews in the vast concentration camp of Auschwitz. What further purpose these murders? It was over; in a few days, all over.

The colonel had heatedly denied there were such murders or had ever been such murders, and as proof offered to take the committee into the presence of the second in command of the entire camp, SS General Wilhelm von Kassel at Birkenau—and the colonel had kept his word. The next day a jeep driven by an SS captain had delivered them—Kassel, Holzer, Jankowski, Stryker, and Stryker's thin, terrified, shivering little girl—to a great stone house where they had waited in a vast bare room. The little girl —he remembered her name, Anna—had wandered off, wandered away somewhere, and then a door had opened and Colonel Kassel invited them into an immense room, an office with many desks, its walls covered with maps, flags, swastikas, and a huge picture of Adolf Hitler.

Standing in the middle of the room, his arms folded across his chest, was a tall, seamed-faced man with arrogant eyes and imperious mien, an officer in full uniform right up to the visored cap on his head. Colonel Kassel, also in full uniform, introduced him.

"My father, General von Kassel." The notorious SS General Wilhelm von Kassel.

Stryker had begun something about his daughter who had disappeared from the outside room—but the general raised a hand and cut him off.

"We're not interested in your damn child. She'll be found." He spoke in German. "Now what in hell do you want here?"

Holzer did the talking, also in German. He began his plea—but Colonel Kassel interrupted, addressing his father. "Tell them we Germans are not wild animals. We have removed the Jews from our society because they are the political enemies of the Third Reich. We have imprisoned them in camps, forced them into labor; yes. But we are not wild animals in a jungle. We do not kill defenseless humans. Tell them."

Wearily the general said, "My son is a fool; an innocent, a fool. Humans!" His voice grated harshly. "Jews—vile, subhuman, enemies of *all* society. We are doing work for the world by obliterating these subhumans. Yes, the war is over; I have received word that allied contingents will be here this very day—but our work does not stop until they stop us! As for these dirty specimens with the temerity to intrude upon their betters—I myself will have the pleasure. . . ." He took his pistol from its holster.

"No!" the son shouted, his own pistol in his hand.

"Fool, stand away." The general leveled his gun.

"No." And the son shot the father, and the father fell, and in the ensuing pandemonium the little girl was there, shrieking, screaming, and Stryker held her to him, her face averted. And it was the colonel himself who assured their safe passage back to Camp No. 6, and it was that day the liberators came, and it was another day, a later day, that Alfred Holzer and Jacob Stryker and Benjamin Jankowski—the little girl by then in a hospital in Australia—testified at Nuremberg.

Colonel Konrad Kassel had taken the stand in his own behalf. He had recited his record with the Luftwaffe, a valiant military record. He had told of his detachment from the Luftwaffe as a full colonel at age twenty-four, and his transfer to Auschwitz as commander of Camp No. 6. He had only been there two months before war's end: he swore he did not know that the transfers of his prisoners to Birkenau meant their transfers to death. He had only found out in those last days, and the killing of his father had been in shock, in reaction. Defense counsel made it clear that in fact it was an heroic act: it had saved the lives of three men whom the father was about to murder. Kassel remained unshaken under pounding cross-examination, and then the sworn story of the three Jews, testifying in behalf of their Nazi captor, sealed his defense. SS Colonel Konrad Kassel, age twenty-four, was acquitted of all crime.

Now there was a knock and Holzer called softly, "Yes, come in."

It was Terry. "Your man's here, Gramps. Downstairs in the drawing room. You want to see him there, or should I bring him up?"

"I'll go down. Thank you, dear."

In the drawing room Dave Jordan introduced himself. He was a tall, dark, pleasant man who politely refused coffee, a sandwich, a drink, and Terry withdrew.

"In a way, Mr. Holzer, I'm a sort of emissary."

"Emissary?" Holzer asked. "What is—emissary? My English, I am quite proud, is good. But I'm afraid—emissary—that good it is not."

"Envoy," Jordan said. "Like a go-between. The middleman."

"Between what—in the middle?"

"I'm to take you to Miss Gaza."

"Oh yes the lady; Rabin told me. Gaza?"

"Juliette Gaza. She's at the Delmonico. We're to be there at two-thirty."

"She's your boss?" Holzer smiled.

"Well . . . yes, in a way."

"Don't look so shy, Mr. Jordan. In Israel the woman has position. Upstairs we have women in government, and downstairs our women are soldiers. You know?"

"I know."

"Look. It's early yet, and such a beautiful day. Unless there's something you want to talk right now . . .?"

"Nothing right now."

"Suppose we walk a little bit. In the sunshine. A beautiful day. Then we grab a cab. All right? You're a young man. You enjoy to walk?"

"Yes."

"Okay? All right?"

"Sure."

Promptly at two-thirty the knock came and Juliette Gaza, refreshed and changed, opened the door for her handsome cohort and a tall, dignified, smiling old man.

"Mr. Holzer?"

"I am Holzer."

"Juliette Gaza." They shook hands. "My pleasure, an extreme pleasure, Mr. Holzer. I've heard so much about you."

"Good or bad?" said the smiling old man.

"All good."

"Thank you." He glanced toward Jordan. "A boss like this I would have thanked God when I was young. I would thank God now."

"I'm not complaining, Mr. Holzer."

"What's *this* all about?" asked Juliette Gaza.

"We were talking, me and Mr. Jordan, about women. I was telling him that when a man is too old to appreciate a beautiful woman, that man is ready to die. I am old, but not ready. I appreciate. You are, if I may say, a very beautiful woman, Miss Gaza."

"Well, thank you."

"Don't mention."

"Is there something I can get you? Send down? A drink? Something?"

"Thank you, nothing."

"Please sit down, Mr. Holzer."

"Thank you." He sat. "I may smoke?"

"Of course."

"Thank you." He took a cigar from a cigar case. He struck a match, let it burn for a moment, then carefully applied the top of the flame to the tip of the cigar. He puffed, settled back. "So? Now?"

Jordan sat, crossed his legs. The lady remained standing.

"Mr. Holzer, my work, our work, Mr. Jordan and myself—it may be a painful experience for you."

"I know what's about. Rabin told me."

"He told you who we are?"

"Shinbet. He told me. If necessary, necessary. To rake up the past, to stir up the dead. . . ."

"Our government thinks it necessary."

"So all right, okay. I am here. God gives compensation. Better an inquisition by a beautiful woman than by an ugly man."

"Not an inquisition, Mr. Holzer. A few questions."

"A *few?*" The old man held away his cigar, European-fashion, between thumb and forefinger, and smiled. "Wanna bet?"

"Please excuse me." She went to the bedroom. From one of the trunks she brought out a small tape recorder, carried it to the sitting room, put it on a table, and sat near it, a distance away from him. "For the record, Mr. Holzer. The present record."

He leaned forward. "A beautiful little instrument. A good one?"

"The best."

"Made in Israel?"

"Made in West Germany."

He puffed his cigar, nodded, sighed, sat back. "Yes, they are very good with machines. So, Miss Gaza?"

"Just a few questions."

"Wanna bet?" The old man grinned. With his own teeth.

She turned on the tape recorder. "We'll begin at the beginning," she said.

She was good. Better than good, he thought. Absolutely brilliant. They're not crazy, the government people, when they send out a woman. Man or woman, makes no difference; they send out the best for whatever the particular job. Brilliant. As good, maybe better, than the vaunted lawyers at the Nuremberg trials. She stabbed in the questions and let him bleed out the answers, and did not interrupt with ego-questions of her own. And in time she got the story, an old story, all of it, and then asked questions that were not even asked back there in the old days.

"What happened to the little girl, Anna Stryker?"

"Collapsed when we got back to the compound, Camp No. 6. A complete nervous breakdown."

"And then? Afterward? What happened to her?"

"She was sent to her grandparents, very old people, in Australia. Stryker had another daughter there, a very little one."

"Gertrude?"

"I don't remember the name."

"Anna Stryker. What happened to her?"

"They put her in a hospital, a sanitarium, an institution."

"For how long?"

"Five years I was told."

"She recovered?"

"From what I heard, yes. I did not hear much. Occasional. Gossip. Rumors. Time passes. Life goes on."

Juliette Gaza was silent, thoughtful. For moments the tape recorder on the table recorded nothing. Alfred Holzer smoked his cigar and admired his inquisitor's legs crossed high.

"Mr. Holzer."

"Miss Gaza?"

"Mr. Holzer, did you—you personally—did you believe that SS Colonel Konrad Kassel, a commander of a camp at Auschwitz—did you believe he was *really* unaware of what was going on around him?"

"I've been asked that question before. Many times."

"I'm asking it now. This time."

"I don't know," Holzer said. "I don't know. Hard to believe —but how not to believe. No proof. Only the other way. Young, a very young man. And he was new, no question—only two months."

"But in those two months, sixty thousand people went from his camp, Camp Number Six, to the ovens at Birkenau. Is it believable he didn't know?"

"That was the court's decision."

"What was *your* decision, Mr. Holzer?"

The old man sighed and smiled toward Jordan. "Look out for them when they're beautiful *and* intelligent. They can be deadly."

"What *was* your decision, Mr. Holzer?" The lady uncrossed her long legs and recrossed them, the skirt even higher. It was distracting.

"Decision," Holzer said, smoked his cigar. "Thank God it was not up to me to make decisions. I'm not trained for those kind of decisions. I'm a man, a diamond-man, a jeweler. I am not a judge." He leaned back, stretched his legs, crossed his ankles, puffed the cigar, blowing smoke at the ceiling. "Hard to believe but not impossible. It just sneaks in *within* the possibility. A young man, a new man, an innocent—a fool, his father called him. And we saw, we witnessed. He saved our lives. We saw a man, a young man, in distraction kill his own father to save the lives of three strangers whom his father was about to murder. We *saw!* My God, we were there, we were it, we were the people. What decision, Miss Gaza? How can *we* think of decisions? He gave us our lives."

"Yes."

And then silence again, a long silence.

"Is there anything you wish to add, Mr. Holzer?"

"What to add? You have taken it all out of me. Only—why? Why, so long after? Why all over again?"

She stood up and he sat forward. She brought him photographs in full color. "Recognize him?"

"You can't miss. Except for the gray in the temples."

"These were quite recently taken."

"Recently. Hard to believe. And so many years. My God, there's hardly a change except for the gray in the hair. He must have had a good life, the colonel, a sweet, easy life."

"The colonel," she said. "Would you please identify him by name, Mr. Holzer? For the tape? These photographs you're looking at—who is he?"

"He is SS Colonel Konrad Kassel, that's who he is."

"Thank you." She took away the pictures. "That's it, Mr. Holzer. The inquisition is over. I do hope it wasn't too bad."

"All right," Holzer said and stood up.

"This is not to be talked about. If you please, not even to your son; nobody. Your government makes that request of you. Yes, Mr. Holzer?"

"All right, okay," he said. "Cloak-and-dagger, our people were *born* into cloak-and-dagger. Read Genesis, read Exodus, even Leviticus, and my God, don't even *begin* on the Talmud. Tell my government all right, okay. I can go now? I am relieved?"

"Thank you. You've been wonderfully helpful."

"Helpful, how? I haven't told you anything I haven't told before. All right, okay, goodbye, good luck."

"Mr. Jordan will take you wherever you wish."

"Who needs your Mr. Jordan? I look like a cripple? I don't need your Mr. Jordan. Goodbye, Mr. Jordan. Goodbye, Miss Gaza. If you need me again, don't hesitate to ask. Give my regards to Mr. Rabin. Tell him for me I said you're a gorgeous woman, Miss Gaza. Goodbye all."

He left a large void. In the stillness she turned off the recorder. "Doughty," she said. "What a wonderful old man."

"Yes," Jordan said. "What happened with the private detective?"

She told him.

"We're just chockful of wonderful old men today," he said.

"Not McGregor. He's no old man."

"Where's that leave us?"

"Marking time, I'm afraid." She yawned. "In rather a short time it's been a long day."

"May I?" he said.

"What?"

"A suggestion."

"What?"

"There isn't much left for us today except—to relax. How about it? Let's have an evening."

"I—I'm tired." She didn't make it sound too convincing.

"Take a nap. I said—evening. In those trunks—not the one with the vents—you happen to have a formal gown?"

"Naturally. Many gowns."

"Let's make an evening. Formal. I'll show you New York. A fine dinner, a fine play. Leave it to me. Anything you like. Yes, Julie?"

"Yes."

"I'll pick you up at seven. I'll bring you an orchid. There's no law says business must prevent pleasure. We have the time for an evening—why not? Yes, Julie?"

"Yes, Dave."

"As Mr. Holzer would say—all right, okay. And also as Mr. Holzer would say." He made a sweeping bow. "Goodbye all."

💀 Ten

McGREGOR hailed a cab, told the man 277 Park Avenue, settled back, lit a cigarette. Shortest distance between two points is a straight line. Shrugged, shook his head. Circuity is the normal method of the sleuth, but when the client is circuitous, the sleuth is robbed of alternative. Inhaled cigarette smoke. Hell, if you live with the lame it does not mean you must limp. She had offered little. His name, business, business address, residential address, photographs. Straight approach might provide a lead to his whereabouts, might also provide information relative to the beautiful client. Beautiful, indubitably, and charming, indubitably, but a liar. Indubitably.

He smoked his cigarette. Certainly she was not constrained to strip herself down to naked truth. On the other hand, if he was being used for a purpose other than the stated purpose, he had a right and duty to pry into that. Right and duty. For himself. Self-preservation. If he was being maneuvered within a matter more complicated than she had admitted, he had a right to know. Because not knowing, you can get hurt, and he was not being paid for risk, he was being paid for a simple trace-job. He could have turned it down, of course. He hadn't. Hell, he was human. Curious. Intrigued. The lady had made an impression. Nevertheless there were tacit conditions. When you buy a detective, you pay your money but you also pay out the pertinent facts. And the withholding of pertinent facts makes you yourself a pertinent fact. Mannheim was prey but she was now quarry. What is fair to the flock is fair to the bird.

277 Park Avenue. A busy lobby. A crowded elevator. And MANNHEIM INCORPORATED in neat gold-leaf letters on a glass door. He opened the door, closed it behind him.

58

"Mr. Mannheim," he said to the young lady at the reception desk.

"Not in," she said.

"Oh?" He put on perturbance. "Somebody. Who's in charge?"

"Mr. Mannheim's assistant, if you wish. Mr. Goritz."

"Sure. Goritz."

"Who shall I say, sir?"

"Personal."

She smiled up at him. "Personal for Mr. Goritz? Or Mr. Mannheim?"

"Mannheim."

"Yessir." She talked into a telephone, hung up, pointed. "Through that door, sir, then it's the second door on the right."

Goritz was a bald little guy with frightened eyes, less than half of him showing in the chair behind a large desk. He stood up and not too much more of him showed. "Yes? What can I do for you? Miss York said personal." He made a little smile around yellow teeth and sat down, and McGregor had his first line on Konrad Mannheim. Mr. Mannheim did not choose to select powerful subordinates.

"Where the hell is he; Mannheim?" It came out sounding the way he wanted it: angry.

"Out of town."

"Where—out of town?"

The frightened eyes blinked. "I don't understand. What is it? Who are you?"

"His wife wants to know."

"Wife?"

"Look, where the hell is he? Where do I get in touch with him?"

"I don't know. Traveling. Out of the country. A buying trip."

"This is home base, isn't it?"

"Yes, his offices."

"Well, you're his assistant, aren't you?" McGregor bellowed.

"Yes, assistant."

McGregor slammed a hand on the desk. "Well, he must let *you* know. When you heard from him last—where was he?"

The little man was quivering. McGregor was huge, and menacing.

"No, I don't know. He hasn't . . . doesn't. . . ."

"When's he coming back?"

"About a month."

"How long away?"

"A couple of weeks."

McGregor backed off, mollified his tone. He felt sorry for the little man. He put apology in his voice. "The wife, she's asking. I'm her fiancé. Name's Jordan."

"Jordan," the little man said, wringing a quavering smile. "The second Jordan today," he said soothingly. "Dave Jordan. Perhaps a relative? He came with Miss Juliette, Gina Juliette from Stuttgart Novelties. Also asking after Mr. Mannheim."

Dave Jordan and Gina Juliette from Stuttgart Novelties. McGregor lit a cigarette. This ground had been covered. He was wasting his time.

"No relation. Coincidence. Me, I—I'm Charles Jordan, Charlie Jordan. Engaged to Mannheim's wife. She's—kinda looking for him."

"Mr. Jordan, Mr. Mannheim doesn't have a wife."

McGregor grinning engagingly. "Ex-wife, I mean. You know?"

"Mr. Mannheim is a bachelor, a life-long bachelor."

Oh the bitch, the beautiful bitch, she sure had put the boots to him, but all within her rights. The private detective isn't the father confessor. Her prerogative, but she must have known sooner or later he'd find out. So what? She had made his job clear to him; what she was paying her money for. To find Mr. Mannheim—and her personal affairs were none of his affair. Well, that's what *you* think, beautiful Miss Gaza. It's like when a witness takes the stand: the personal life is open to inspection. In this case when I work for you I'm linked to you, and I must know a bit of your motivation in order that I myself not be in jeopardy. We'll be playing games with each other, Miss Gaza, but my side is reaction to your action: you started the game.

McGregor squinted, bumbled oafish. "Mr. Goritz, I may be in the wrong place, at the wrong time, all wrong. Your boss—Bruce Mannheim?"

"Konrad Mannheim."

"Golly *gee,* am I all wrong! Shows you, love makes you a little nuts. She tells me Mannheim, she tells me he's the president of a big corporation, I look up a Mannheim corporation in the phone book, and I wind up all wet and all wrong. Golly gee. I crave your pardon, sir. A thousand pardons."

"Not at all. Not at all, Mr. Jordan." Goritz drew out a handkerchief and wiped his face.

"You'll forgive me, sir? Please forgive me."

The little man was squeaking in relief. The huge madman was somewhat sane. And soon he'd be rid of him. What an experience. "Of course, of course, Mr. Jordan. We—we—we all make mistakes." He stood up and came around the desk, handkerchief loose in his fist like a trailing plume. "Yes. Love. I know." The hand without the handkerchief touched McGregor's elbow, and he led him toward the door. "I—I trust you'll find your man, the right one. Haste makes—you know—whatever. Slowly. Search slowly and I'm sure you'll find him."

"Thank you, Mr. Goritz, and forgive the intrusion. Slowly. Yes. Good advice. You're most kind. And understanding. You've been a brick." He clapped the little man on the shoulder and the little man shuddered. "Love. Eh. Well, goodbye, Mr. Goritz."

Five minutes to three. The sun from the west making long easterly shadows along Central Park South. No. 218 was tall and narrow. No doorman. 218—the second and last stop on the straightline deal, then home to shower, shave, dress, and on to Café Ulrich, the Wine and Food Society, the Confrerie des Chevaliers du Tastevin, and Tillie.

The first stop had been amusing—he chuckled—and not entirely unproductive. It had opened three aspects within the area of preliminary investigation. Number One—the nature of the man he was hunting. Konrad Mannheim was a loner, and a hard-ego type. When the first assistant to·the president of a corporation is a squeaking, perspiring, submissive little fellow, then the president is not one to delegate authority, and when you don't share authority in business then simply you do not share authority, business, personal, or otherwise. Which makes you a loner, which is a hard-ego type, which, if you're successful or even mildly successful

(Mannheim Incorporated; his own name right up there) stamps self-sufficiency all over you and marks you a dangerous opponent. Number Two—the opponent has not been in town for the past two weeks and will not be for the next four weeks, or so at least had Mr. Goritz been instructed and so he believed. No fabrication there. The pipsqueak lost behind (protected by?) his impressive desk had blurted truth (or what he believed to be the truth). And Number Three—corroboration that the comely client was a thoroughly untrustworthy bitch (at least in connection with her detective).

So, McGregor, what in hell are you doing *here?* Four o'clock you have an appointment with Tillie Ulrich. Why this second port of call? And shrugged in the sunlight and smiled across at the trees in the park. Again a multiple answer, but only two parts this time. One—the little fellow in the office believed the boss to be traveling, somewhere out of the country, but belief does not make gospel. Could possibly be that's what the boss wanted him to believe. Could possibly be the boss was shacking right here in his flat, a six-week vacation at home but away from business, phone turned off, in this fine old soundproof building, not one of the new ones with the auditory walls where even the sounds of love had to be hushed. Two—the pipsqueak had pronounced the boss a life-long bachelor. Well, now. A life-long bachelor is wont to have on occasion—the occasion sometimes attentuating to a long celebration—a playmate. The playmate is sometimes shucked off to an apartment of her own for which you pay the rent (and sundry other monies going to her total upkeep) or is shacked in your apartment, making hay or in the hay while you are out of the country for six weeks on a buying trip. Shucked or shacked—it was worth a try, but he was no longer—grinning—disguised as the fiancé of an ex-wife. So? Just in case there was an answer—who was he? The doorbell rings, the door opens—who am I? Depends. *If* the door opens—who opens the door. If it opens, I'll make it fit. "Suit the action to the word, the word to the action." Worst comes to worst I can always holler detective.

He quit the sunshine for a long, cool, quiet, narrow, immaculate lobby. There was a stairway in the rear and a self-service elevator in front. The indicator showed fifteen stories to the building, the elevator resting on the third floor. He thumbed the button for service and the elevator came down to him. Inside he tapped the 4-button and the elevator ascended silently.

The fourth floor was like the lobby: long, narrow, quiet, immaculate. He swiveled a look to either end: only two apartments to a floor, one in front, one in back. That made them, in this neighborhood, expensive. And exclusive. And—no doorman downstairs—very private. So already, second stop in the preliminary investigation, not a loss. Another bead had been added to his string on Mannheim. The man lived on a fine street, lived expensively, and liked his privacy.

4A was to the front, facing the park. He touched the doorbell and almost immediately there was a response. A voice. Thick, male, guttural, grumbling in German. McGregor knowing a bit of the language was able to make out:

". . . am I also a servant that I must wait upon doors . . . ?"

The lock snapped. The door opened.

The man was big, blond, crew-cut, with a neat Van Dyke beard, and a scar not unhandsome over the right cheekbone. But the eyes. Nervous, darting, they viewed McGregor in absolute shock. Worse, terror. And then the door swung shut with force, but McGregor had his foot in, and it bounced back, and he thrust at the broad chest of the burly man who stumbled back and now it was McGregor who kicked shut the door but he stood stock-still because of the gun. Huge, gleaming. Looked like a Luger. Quite competently held, except the hand holding it was trembling. Not good, not salubrious. Certainly not conducive to pacific conversation. A lethal weapon, a trembling hand, terrified eyes.

"Now look here, mister, don't. . . ."

The click of misfire saved his life and he did not wait for correction. He leaped, hard, low, and they fell, but McGregor, a career man in Homicide, was holding the hand holding the gun, and even as they thrashed in struggle a section of his mind was laughing at himself for getting just deserts from having taken on a client he knew was lying to him, and then the gun went off and the odor of the cordite filled the room and the thick body beneath him became inert.

Panting, on his knees, McGregor looked at a corpse with a gun still in its hand, a rivulet of blood flowing from the small hole, a contact wound in the right temple. Without hope he put his ear to

63

the man's heart and of course, nothing. He sighed, stood up, moved about, inspecting. Five rooms. Two bedrooms, a living room, a dining room, a kitchen—but Konrad Mannheim no longer lived in apartment 4A at 218 Central Park South. He had moved out totally, entirely, irrevocably, kit and kaboodle. Every closet was empty, every drawer bare.

Returning to the living room McGregor hoped for better in his search through the dead man's clothes but was only slightly rewarded. No wallet, no paper of identification. Thirty-nine dollars in bills, sixty-seven cents in change, a claim check to the baggage room at Grand Central Station, and a key. Pocketing the claim check, he tested the key in the door. Of course. That's how the guy had got in. Who was he? Why was he here? An appointment —no question he had had an appointment right here in the apartment. He had answered the door-ring without even inquiring. But he had grumbled. ". . . am I also a servant that I must wait upon doors . . . ?" Then he had expected the appointee to have a key of his own. Or her own.

McGregor paced, squinting, pondering. Mannheim? A messenger of Mannheim's? A sweetheart of Mannheim's? Perhaps even the complicated Miss Juliette Gaza. Or, turning it around, perhaps none of them. Perhaps Mannheim had passed along the empty apartment to the man with the Van Dyke and the appointment was with some crony of his own, perhaps someone with whom he was going to share the apartment. Or, turning it all the way around again, perhaps there was no appointment at all: ratiocination has its limitations. But in any event he, McGregor, did not belong in apartment 4A pacing the carpet with a dead man on the living room floor.

He went to the door, looked back. All quite peaceful. The thick-weave carpet showed no sign of a struggle and nothing was overturned. He went out, locked the door with the key, and pushed the button for the elevator.

Downstairs in the fresh air, as he looked at his watch, new problems crowded in on him. Should he disappoint Tillie (and himself), give up the long-awaited once-a-year dinner, and station himself as lookout here in the vicinity for the rest of the day (and night)? No, he was too old for wild goose chasing. Even on the off-chance that it *was* Mannheim coming back to the empty apart-ment—so what? He had neither the right nor the authority to pounce on him, detain him, arrest him. As far as he knew, Mann-heim was a perfectly respectable business man; even Juliette Gaza had said no word to the contrary. But if he did show up—he could tail him. Could he? McGregor, no amateur, knew the ex-treme difficulties of a one-man tail-job. If the man came in a car, he had no car to follow him. Finding a taxi in that split-second was as likely as finding sunshine in a coal mine. And if the man took a taxi, the same applied. Further, if it *was* Mannheim he would be coming out after finding a dead man in his apartment. Certainly he would be wary. McGregor, no amateur, knew the ease with which a man if so bent could slip a tail. No. If Konrad Mannheim *were* in town, if he was *not* out of the country on a buying trip—there were professional ways of tracking him down. And if he were out of the country there were also professional ways, but it would take a bit more time. McGregor, pleased to be attending the Wine and Food Society dinner, dismissed that prob-lem and went on to the others.

The guy up there was some kind of nut. A nice ordinary citizen isn't host to a gun and doesn't use it that quickly. Whoever he was he was a guy on the *qui vive,* possibly a criminal; terror had blazed in his eyes at the sight of a stranger and the finger on the trigger had not waited for explanations. If he was connected with Mannheim then Mannheim was connected with a loon. Time, on that. We'll see. The claim check ought to help. Funny if Gaza was really seeking the loon. They do go roundabout like that when they come to the private detectives, especially the ones who are large with fee. For five thousand bucks this was not a routine trace-job.

But loon or not, the guy up there was dead and you can't let him rot. The impulse to be stemmed of course was to report it to the cops. A dead guy in the apartment would open up Mannheim to the cops and that wouldn't be quite cricket to the client. The lady had retained a confidential agent to turn up Mannheim pri-vately, not to explode him to the cops. So—discretion. Where was it written?—"O discretion, thou art a jewel!"

Upstairs in 4A lay a chap with a beard, pistol in hand, contact wound in his right temple. Plainly a suicide. If a caller were expected and the caller had a key, the suicide would be reported and the gentlemen of the gendarmerie would upset Miss Gaza by raising brouhaha re Konrad Mannheim. If not—if either the caller did not have a key or there were no caller at all—McGregor would know. He would return during the night. If the chap with the beard were still on the carpet he would get him and lay him out somewhere and tip it in anonymously to the nearest precinct house.

He had his hand up for a cab—and let it fall. No! If the chap with the beard were indeed to be considered a suicide—how had he gotten in if he did not have a key on his person?

With a last lugubrious glance at his watch McGregor set out quickly for the corner, made the turn down Sixth Avenue, sought a hardware store, found one, and smoked impatiently while a duplicate key was made for him. Then back to 218 where he rang the bell, this time, downstairs. No answer. Upstairs he rang the bell again, no answer, and entered into the acrid smell of the cordite. He slipped the key into a pocket of the dead man's jacket, and went out and locked the door with the new key. In the street he got a cab to Grand Central Station where he presented the claim check and received in exchange a heavy leather suitcase.

He took a cab home.

He put the suitcase in a corner of his bedroom.

Ah, time, time, fled, sped. Dear Tillie.

He showered, shaved, dressed—all took time.

He arrived at Café Ulrich an hour and a half late—five-thirty —to effusive greetings from old friends but only a nod from Tillie, cold, stern, uncomprehending, disappointed.

> Love, friendship, charity, are subjects all
> To envious and calumniating time.
>
> How my achievements mock me!

66

℞ Eleven

KONRAD MANNHEIM. Sitting slumped behind the wheel of the rented car on the Fifty-ninth Street Bridge. Stuck. Traffic motionless. Twenty minutes now. But soon, soon now, was the word relayed back. When at first the cars had stopped he had believed it to be a normal delay, but after five minutes he had got out and inquired of the driver in front of him, who had inquired of the driver in front of him, and that one of the one in front of him, and so the drivers of the long line of cars going into the city had learned of the accident on the Manhattan end of the bridge, a pile-up. Ambulances were coming, and tow trucks. On either side of the bridge, police were rerouting traffic, but those cars already bumper to bumper on the bridge would simply have to wait until there was clearance at the Manhattan end. Turn off your motors and wait, the police had instructed. And now the word had drifted back: soon. Soon they would be moving again.

He was impatient but philosophical. Not a plight, a delay; at this stage in matters another harassing delay, but nothing critical. Lubeck would wait. He would have preferred to be waiting for Lubeck, but first in Montreal there had been a delay in the plane flight, and now this here on the bridge. But Lubeck would wait. It was not as though they were meeting on some street corner. Lubeck had a key and would be comfortable in the apartment.

Lubeck comfortable? Exaggeration. Lubeck was never comfortable, because he was sick. In the head. In the spirit. In the soul. Lubeck was a mad, shrewd, stupid, inconsolable son of a bitch and therefore dangerous, but that danger was a part of the full consideration. Lubeck's madness, Gertrude's quirks—all a part of the grand plan. Grand Plan. He chuckled. Actually the small plan before the grand plan with the *Blau Gruppe,* with

67

friends and constituents in Germany. Return of the exile. Already the political underworld of the Fatherland was seething with rumors. Return from exile, albeit a self-imposed exile. The moment had come. The time was ripe. After the long patience—the return. In the very nature of politics—charisma.

He tapped out a cigarette from a pack, lit it. Gauloises. For an international man it was chic to smoke Gauloises and he liked being chic but that was not the point. He preferred American cigarettes but his smoking Gauloises was another of his symbols: he hated Americans and all things American. Gauloises. He looked at the cigarette as he blew smoke at it. He also hated the French, but they were minor. The Americans were the conquerors. The worst kind of conquerors. Conquerors who smashed you, then picked up your pieces and pasted you together and fondled and nurtured you—despicable pretense. They razed your cities. They killed your women and children. And now they loved you —because it was expedient. Because your power was their bulwark against the Red Bear in the East whose fingers they now were licking because they were afraid. Well, it was time once again they were afraid of *us*. They have heaped kindness upon us, oppressive kindness, dividing us, suppressing us as a nation; they have given us their gold and taken away our pride, our nationalism. Well, we are ready to take our proper place in the orbit of first class powers. We are ready to reject the political panderers who are now our leaders. We are ready, *Gross Amerikanisch Schwein,* to turn over the table you have set for us.

A last puff and he threw out the cigarette, ruminating the present, the immediate situation. He would not, ever, return to Mannheim Incorporated on Park Avenue in New York. There was the small office in Bonn that would grow to be the big office, and once he was finally quit of America he would order the fool Goritz to wind up his American affairs. For the world—except for that one day last week—he was in Canada. Even today, especially today, for the world he was in Canada. When he would finally return to New York to go to the bank vault, that would be open, above-board and hasty, and then back to Canada and the flight to Germany—his effects were already transported—and then it would be finished here and the new beginning begun in the homeland. He smiled, plucked out another cigarette, lit it.

He was registered in a small hotel in Montreal and continually made open appearances there and would again later today. The flight to New York was only an hour. He had slipped out by a side exit. The flight back, an hour. Simple to stroll in inconspicuously. And every day, even today, he had made purchases in Canada for shipment to his warehouse in New Jersey. The first and only unexpected incident had been the presence of Gertrude's sister in the apartment in Flushing. Impelled by nagging desire, he had appeared without notice, intending to sleep over. What else was she good for, except business, his beautiful Jewess? The sister was there but his clever *Jude* had managed superbly. Oh my, my ex-boss from Mannheim Incorporated! To what, sir, do I owe the honor? She had played it beautifully for this sister arrived from Sydney, Australia, and he had stayed for an hour drinking with his always-drinking Gertrude, and had left frustrated but thankful for the wisdom, the sophistication, the perspicuity of his Jewess inamorata.

Gertrude the beautiful. A dichotomy in the soul of Konrad Mannheim. Physically a pleasure, spiritually an abomination. She had come to him as a business secretary eighteen months ago, Gertrude Stryker. Stryker. The name had brought a surge of memory and a smile of satisfaction. So long ago, how well it had gone. But there were many Strykers all over the world, Gertrude from Australia, and she had come with a fine letter of recommendation from none other than Hermann Koblentz. Koblentz, high and respected, a lieutenant-general during the war and an official of government after the war. And so a year and a half ago this beautiful Stryker from Australia had come to him as a secretary and six months later had been retired. He had arranged the little apartment in Flushing, and had promised marriage. Marriage—when the time came. Marriage—when Konrad Mannheim was finally elevated to his just position. Marriage in the homeland, the Fatherland, when the time came, to a Jewess despite any objection from the old Germans—he was a new German. And she had served him faithfully and well, traveling with him to Germany and Argentina as a trusted companion and amanuensis. She knew of his dealings with Ludwig Lubeck and knew of and sanctioned his plan for Lubeck but did not know of his plan for her.

Dispensable. Both of them. And when he returned to Montreal

this day he could prove by plotted, devious method that Konrad Mannheim had been all this day out on business or inside his hotel room, had been all this day, as on the other days, in Montreal, Canada. Who knows who is a passenger on a quick flight from Montreal to New York and back? Who knows of any connection between Konrad Mannheim and Ludwig Lubeck? Gertrude Stryker knows, but she is the only one who knows and she will not be able to say.

A million dollars in American money. Completely isolated from Lubeck's embezzlement, Konrad Mannheim was, at most, a friend of Lubeck's. If worst came to worst, he had given Lubeck a key to his apartment. Lubeck was coming to America and he Mannheim was leaving America—and so he had turned over his apartment to Lubeck for the term of his lease. The money was already here in a vault in Mannheim's name and Lubeck thought he was protected because he had the key to the vault. A part of their deal, protection for each of them: the vault in Mannheim's name under Mannheim's signature, but the key in Lubeck's possession. The idiot, the foreigner, the damned Argentinian idiot. Mannheim had prayed it would work and it *had* worked—Lubeck believed that his key to the vault was the only key; he did not know that *two* keys were given to the owner of an American vault. Gertrude knew. Gertrude knew all, but—not all. Today was the day. Penultimate.

They would talk in the apartment, he and Lubeck, and then Lubeck would take a hotel room and there Mannheim would accomplish it. The pistol was in his pocket, a .22, and the silencer. No one could possibly know except Gertrude, and Gertrude would not be available to say. First Lubeck, then Gertrude, and Konrad Mannheim would be back in Montreal. Gertrude had rented the car in her own name and had waited for him in the car at La Guardia. Even now he was wearing gloves, there could not be an imprint, no fingerprints. He would leave the car in front of Gertrude's apartment house. Then a cab to the airport and the quick flight to Montreal where he would then make his presence known. In the event of any question—what possible connection to two murders in one day in New York City? He had been in Montreal all day, at work or resting in his hotel room. And what possible motive could Konrad Mannheim have? Lubeck was an acquaintance from Argentina, Gertrude a friend in Flushing. And the way he planned it, Gertrude would not be discovered for days, perhaps weeks, and so the two murders would be divided in time and not linked. Yes, that was quite possible.

If ever he were closely questioned about Gertrude, he would admit they had once been lovers but it was over—and the way it had worked itself out he actually had a form of proof. The sister! That day last week when he had come into New York—he would say it was to pick up the last of his clothes and things from the apartment—he had dropped in for a short visit with his former sweetheart. The sister was there. She was a witness, a corroboration of the fact that Gertrude had been formal and distant and quite surprised at the visit from her former employer. He had stayed for a short while, himself formal and distant, and left.

In point of fact when driving in from La Guardia earlier he had asked Gertrude about the sister—in a sense important to him, an ally—but Gertrude (always somehow faintly smelling of whisky) had shrugged off his questions and had talked about the business of Lubeck, and had talked about him and her and their marriage when he was finally permanently settled in Germany and would send for her. She believed him to be in love with her, the abominable *Jude* whose brains and body he had used, and even more the shrewd Jew bitch believed she had him trussed and tied like an animal to be dispatched for slaughter. Blackmail. Subtle blackmail. With all she knew about him, he could not risk rejecting her.

He had delivered her to her apartment house, kissed her cheek, and driven off in the rented car—rented by her in her name. Even that was part of the plan. Under his instruction she had rented the car for a month, a full month, and had taken it a week ago. That did not make this particular day pertinent, and they would not come to inquire about the car for another three weeks. There was no one else (except now possibly the sister) and he had told Gertrude to tell the sister (his excuse the exigencies of present events) that she might go away for a few weeks on vacation. No one else. She had no friends, no callers, no visitors—no one would try her door.

That, in fact, had been an inspiration. To leave her door unlatched and unlocked and to say, in the event of inquiry, that that

71

was a practice of hers, careless—she drank, frequently forgot to snap the lock; the door could be opened by the turn of the knob. It could explain an intrusion, and consequent murder.

Carefully he tamped out his cigarette, carefully deposited it in the dashboard ashtray. He must remember, after, to touch the snap-button of the lock, to leave the door open. She would not be discovered for days, possibly weeks, and the way he planned it the body would be preserved unputrefied.

All else was in order. Today, after the work to be done, he would return to Montreal—only an hour's journey—and make himself cheerfully evident in the taproom of the hotel and the nightclubs of the town. As a matter of fact he had a date with a lovely young girl, a Montreal *poule*. And then, in a couple of weeks, the unobtrusive return to New York to the bank vault, and then the flight from Canada to Germany and at long last, permanently, home. Plus! Plus one million dollars in cold, hard, American cash. It would help. Oh, it would help! There is nothing like money in a campaign for public office.

Motors churned, cars started. The traffic moved.

He found a space not far from 218, parked accurately, precisely. He walked to 218, took the elevator to the fourth floor, rang his doorbell and received no response. Good. If Lubeck was late, that would make *him* early. He prided himself on accuracy, promptitude, precision. The short delay of the Montreal to New York flight, the long tie-up on the bridge—not his fault and not within his reckonings however propitiative.

He used his key, turned the double lock, entered and saw immediately beyond the small foyer the body on the living room floor. He stiffened, stood rigid. Then he turned the lock and proceeded by short, tentative, tiptoe-steps to Ludwig Lubeck on the living room floor. He looked down at Lubeck, then looked about the room. Luggage. Where was his luggage? He went to the bedrooms, the dining room, returned to the living room—no luggage. Now he bent to one knee examining but not touching.

He noted the Luger tightly clenched in the right hand. He noted the powder burns surrounding the hole in the right temple. The muzzle had been pressed close, a contact wound. Blood was a smear on the right side of the face. Coagulated blood was a splotch in the right ear. And that was it. Nothing else. No blood on the carpet. He stood up tall over the body, wanted to spit at it, restrained himself.

Dead, the son of a bitch, by his own hand. But, somehow, not unexpected. A mean man, narrow, riddled with guilt, and at last, at final, it had been too much. Rotten, neurotic, suspicious, tormented. The deed finally done, a massive robbery accomplished, it had overwhelmed him. But the swine had had a need to draw in his partner. Guilt. Transference. Neurotic expiation. He killed himself here, passing along the guilt. Always with neurotics someone else is to blame. I did not kill myself. You killed me. By going along with me, encouraging me, offering me protection, you brought me to this pass. Here I am, dead. You killed me.

No luggage. Which meant he had registered in a hotel somewhere before coming to the apartment for his final scene. The weak, weird, miserable son of a bitch. Hotel key?

He knelt and searched the clothes. No hotel key. Probably left it at the desk wherever in hell he had registered. Nothing in the clothes but the key to this apartment and a bit of money. He took the key and the money, stood up. This murder had been done for him. In bad circumstances, but done. It would require a shift in plan, an acceleration. The money in the bank vault was now all his, without possible demurrer. He would come back sometime this week, pick it up, exchange his reservation to Germany for an earlier date and be quickly away, home, and out of all this. Now the body. Disposition.

He would carry it out but he could not carry it far. All right. In the entire building there were only thirty apartments and none of the tenants, unless by reason of emergency, used the stairway. He would carry it down and leave it behind the stairs on the ground floor. There they would find him, his pockets empty, another victim of another mugging, shot to death from up close. If there was inquiry of the tenants of the building, at least one of them, Konrad Mannheim, it would be learned by contact with his office, was away on a buying trip.

He opened the door, looked out into the hall. Quiet. Empty.

He came back to the living room, took the gun from the clenched fist and pocketed it. He lifted the body, slung it over his shoulder, opened the door, quickly carried it to the stairway. The bastard was heavy, but it was only four floors. Breathless, he deposited Ludwig Lubeck behind the stairs in the rear on the ground floor, went to the front to the elevator, touched the button with a gloved finger. Upstairs he looked over the apartment. Nothing. Excellent. He went out, locked the door with the key that had been in Lubeck's clothes, and outside in the sunshine crossed into the park. There by the lake he found a place alone, casually tossed the Luger into the water. Then quite sprightly he returned to Gertrude's rented car. He put the key in the ignition, turned the motor, and drove toward Flushing in the Borough of Queens in the City of New York.

℘ Twelve

SHE drank too much, that she admitted. That she was an alcoholic she refused to admit. She had never had a blackout, she had never fallen, never made a spectacle of herself; she functioned perfectly. True, there were days she drank before breakfast; true, she was a solitary drinker (but a solitary drinker is no more than a social drinker who drinks alone when so disposed); and true the damned liquor was a crutch for her. Yes she drank too much she admitted, but there are those of us—each of us is different—with the kind of constitution that can take it.

She looked up from her cleaning (*he* was coming and for him the apartment must be spotless); she looked at a mirror and had to smile. Even disheveled and without makeup, she was beautiful. In all modesty, beautiful. In all modesty an acknowledged beauty: in high school she had won the contests and reigned as beauty queen and then in college each year of the four years she had been voted beauty queen against all the tall, towering Australian girls. She was tiny, one hundred and three pounds soaking wet but all of it perfectly proportioned, and in all the years—not so many, really—she had not gained more than half a pound. *Ma petite* he called her in his German-accented French.

They say alcohol takes a toll, it makes ravages; well, it had not ravaged her. Even Anna, who had not seen her in two years, had said she was absolutely unchanged. Anna.

She shuddered, went quickly to the glass on the coaster on the table, the fourth such glass already today: a tall glass with Scotch on ice and a dash of bitters and a touch of vermouth and a shard of lemon peel and a splash of water. She sipped, held the glass away, dourly smiled at it. There are those of us who need you. Some take dope. There are those of us who from our very beginning require a crutch. An orphan reared by elderly grandparents. In a country where the language was English, she had spoken only German until she was four. And then the arrival of an older sister—old?—Anna was only eleven then, thin, weak, meek, silent, something wrong with her. They had put her away in a hospital, a crazy one in a mental institution—nervous breakdown, the grandparents had explained; the poor child, all she had been through—and Anna had not come out for five long years, still the silent one who never talked of her experiences during the war.

She had, deep inside of her, been afraid of Anna: to her Anna was "the crazy one" despite the fact the doctors, the psychiatrists, said she was fully recovered. And when the grandparents had died it was Anna who had taken her in and cared for her; she had lived with her but somehow fearful, somehow always deep inside afraid of the crazy one. Yet it was Anna who had married, not Gertrude.

Beauty queen. A curse. No man was ever good enough, no one deserved her. She slept with many and drank with many and married none. But Anna married—another silent one, tall, thin, gaunt, burning-eyed, an older man, a German from the old country, an economist, Herr Doktor Hermann Koblentz. He had been a high officer in the German army, and a high official with the postwar government in Bonn, and had come to Australia for reasons of health and was a professor in the university there. But even in marriage Anna took care of the little sister: she insisted Gertrude move in with them. She did, but it was not charity. She contributed her share to the household. She was earning good wages as a private secretary.

Then Herr Doktor took sick, tuberculosis, and was away in a sanitarium for six months and when he came home she knew it was finished. A crazy one *and* a sick one, it was time to get out. She made her plans, made her arrangements, and then announced her decision. She was going to America, to New York. Anna pleaded, the silent husband listening, but Gertrude was adamant. When they realized her decision was final, they gave her their blessings—and money, a nest-egg for emergencies in the foreign country. She remembered a conversation, a day before her departure, with the professor in his office at the university.

"Gertrude, this is strictly between us. I prefer that Anna know nothing of this."

"Why?"

"It has to do with Germany, the war period, a bad time for Anna. You understand?"

"Yes, but no. Germany? The war period? Why?"

"It is for you. To help you, possibly. A recommendation to a man in America." The professor smiled. "In a way, he owes you."

"Me? I know him?"

"No. I know him. Knew him when I was an officer in the army, and after. Here." He gave her an envelope. "It is a recommendation. To . . . Konrad Mannheim, now a successful business man in New York. Mannheim Incorporated, Two-seventy-seven Park Avenue, New York City. Tell him you're my sister-in-law. He once had a great respect for me, probably still has. I'm certain he'll give attention to a recommendation from me."

"Thank you."

In America, also on recommendation, she had taken a room in a girls' hotel, and a week after arrival had presented herself at the offices of Mannheim Incorporated. She had been interviewed, quite cordially, by Kurt Goritz, who had first taken Dr. Koblentz's letter of recommendation into Mr. Mannheim's private office.

"You speak German, Miss Stryker?"

"Fluently."

"And can take dictation in German?"

"Of course."

"And naturally in English?"

"Of course."

"Mr. Mannheim is quite interested, Miss Stryker, but at the moment—not."

"I don't understand."

"Well, Mr. Mannheim's secretary, personal secretary, she has, well, rather recently, married, and, when one marries, you know, there is, well, the possibility, probability, of a family. Are you married, Miss Stryker?"

"No."

"If you will please leave your address and phone number . . ."

That had been two years ago.

Two years.

She drank now, a deep draught, and returned to cleaning, polishing, fixing the apartment. Two years. For the first six months she had changed jobs three times, boring jobs three times, and always the men, no different from the men in Sydney, desiring, wanting. She had given to some of them but never with love. In all her life the beauty queen had not had love.

And then, after six months, the call had come.

"Mr. Mannheim would like to talk with you, Miss Stryker. If you're still available."

She had tried to sound hard. "Well, that depends. . . ."

"Mr. Mannheim is very much interested and I assure you he's most liberal salary-wise. May I arrange the interview?"

"Yes."

A year and a half now. For the first time in her life in love. Deeply, desperately, totally committed. Dearest God, I *love* him. During the initial period, unlike any of the others, he had seemed oblivious—despite all her little tricks. A boss. Kind, polite, considerate, appreciative, charming, always charming. But not a move. Not a hint. Not one action. And she had pined. Like a youngster. An adolescent. Lost in puppy love. During that initial period she had had her full share of dates but had been childishly, spitefully, stupidly faithful, had not gone to bed with one of them. And then that day, dear God finally that day, when he had asked if she could work with him in the evening, if she were free that evening. Yes, she was free that evening. Would she consider coming—it was important—say eight o'clock to his apartment? Of course, Mr. Mannheim. You know the address, Miss Stryker? I do. Two-eighteen Central Park South? Yessir, I know. Eight o'clock, Miss Stryker? Yes, Mr. Mannheim.

He had taken her at once. Almost without preliminary. He had offered champagne and she had drunk it although she hated champagne. There had been no pretext of office business, no mewling male pretense. He had attacked and she had accepted. He had taken her right there on the living room floor with their clothes on, and then naked in his bedroom in bed, and he had been all she had dreamed he would be, a beautiful knowing man, superb. And then they had slept, satisfied sleep, and then again in darkness, wonderful love-making, and then a long deep sleep and then in the pale morning they had talked, lovers in love, and he was all the man she had hoped against all hope he would be. No cheap affair. Not business and bedroom and discharge at surfeit. No.

I love you, Gertrude. So stupid the words as I hear them, my saying them. After so long. All these months.

I love you.

All these months. Like a sickness. I—I didn't dare.

Yes. Like a sickness. Nor I. Didn't dare. My dear God. Yes. I. Never in my life said it before. I love you, Mr. Mannheim.

Mr. Mannheim. Konrad. Say Konrad.

I—I can't.

Say I love you, Konrad.

I love you, Konrad.

Again.

I love you. Konrad.

You're fired. As of now. We'll miss you in the office. I'll miss you. Goritz will miss you. I couldn't live like that. You in the office every day. Please. You understand?

Yes. I think.

We'll get someone. There's always someone.

I'll stay and help. The new someone.

Never.

Mr. Goritz. What'll he think? Mr. Goritz?

Goritz. Let him die. Say it.

What?

Say I love you, Konrad.

I love you, Konrad. Dear God. I do.

For three weeks she lived with him while he hunted an apartment for her. She lived and loved in 218 until he found her own apartment for her in Flushing, Queens. She moved in quietly, settled quietly. He paid for everything, the furniture, everything; he bought her gifts, gave her money, she had quite a substantial bank account. He earned a good living but he was not in fact a wealthy man; the money from Argentina, from the National Socialist League, would at long last make him free of money worry, independently rich.

She lived quietly, that was the theme. What with a political career looming ahead in Germany he must at all costs avoid scandal here in America. No one (except Lubeck) knew about them. He was discreet, she was not gregarious. He wrote no letters to her, she had no writings of his. He kept no clothes in her apartment, she kept no clothes in his. She had no friends, she cared about nobody but him; even her telephone number was unlisted. When they traveled they lived apart: Miss Gertrude Stryker was his personal secretary.

Lubeck knew about them because Konrad wanted it that way: a sign of trust to the ever-suspicious Lubeck. On three different occasions Lubeck had had dinner here, right here in the apartment, because Konrad wanted it that way. "A home-cooked meal for my friend Ludwig." A family meal for Lubeck who had no family, no relatives, no children: he had been married as a youth and was long ago divorced.

Lubeck. Even now, right now. . . .

To hell with Lubeck. She went to her glass, drank. As an accomplice with full knowledge she was as much a murderer as Konrad. To hell with it. To hell with everything, everyone—only Konrad was important. For once in her life she was totally committed, totally engaged, bewitched, in love, and beyond the point of morals, pride, or conscience. Accomplice to murder? God, she *was* a murderer. And she would never tell him. And if he didn't know by now—he in Canada when the tiny notices appeared in the New York papers—he would never know. It was finished in the public prints. Another unimportant death of an another unimportant person in a vast country of 200,000,000 souls. And soon he would be permanently away in Germany and once settled and established there he would send for her.

Soon. Soon.

She drank.

Anna.

In Sydney the tubercular husband had died and Anna had re-assumed her maiden name. She had gone back to work despite the fact that she was the beneficiary of a large insurance policy, but the work had not served the purpose. Her letters to Gertrude told of unhappiness alone in old familiar surroundings, and then the letter had arrived telling of Anna's new plans. She was going to move to Israel and live out her life there. She would first come to America for a six-month visit, and then on to Israel.

Gertrude herself found the apartment for Anna atop the steep stairway on the first floor of 523 East 47th Street, a charming little furnished apartment, and undistracted because Konrad was away in Canada had played the good sister. And why not? Anna the quiet, the crazy one, had been kind to her all her life. She had told Anna she was between jobs and had plenty of free time.

And then that evening in the apartment here, last Thursday evening entertaining Anna with a put-together dinner of American delicatessen, had come the ring, Konrad's ring—two short and one long—and she had flown to the door before he could use his key.

Konrad the beautiful. Tall and straight and slender. Suave, not at all discomposed at the unexpected presence of the sister, always the man of the world, giving no hint of displeasure, he had been charming, aloofly attentive, exactly playing his part. My ex-boss! What a nice surprise! And after a few drinks and fit-and-start conversation—what conversation with a withdrawn Anna, always silent but grown so terribly pale; did she realize the dissimulation, suspect the true nexus between them?—he had taken his leave to her own deep disappointment. Had he but waited, tarried longer, she would have gotten rid of Anna. But not Konrad, wise Konrad. He took no chances.

And at once on his departure, Anna pleaded to go home. She wasn't feeling well. Migraine. She was nauseated. And she had driven her to the city in the rented car—rented at his behest and she knew for what purpose: it was being used for its purpose right now—and all the way into town Anna had not said a word, not unusual with quiet Anna, the strange one, the crazy one. She had left her at 523 East 47th Street, promising to return at 10:30 Saturday morning for the day of shopping they had talked about before Konrad had come.

No word from Anna on Friday. She had called twice: no answer from Anna. And that day Konrad had called from Canada, voicing disappointment at not being able to be with her Thursday night but affable, thoroughly comprehending the situation, the visiting sister, and had advised her on the sister. "After Lubeck it's possible I might need you, possible I might want you here for a time, I mean here in Canada not here in this hotel. I wouldn't want her to worry with you away. Tell her you're planning to go away on vacation for a few weeks; tell her that just in case, just to cover if necessary. Yes?"

"Yes, Konrad."

"You know when to pick me up at the airport. The Lubeck business."

"Yes, Konrad."

"Goodbye for now. I love you. See you then."

And on Saturday the bombshell had burst. Anna drinking. In the morning. Anna of all people and drinking of all things—gin. Anna Stryker drinking gin at 10:30 in the morning, and Anna talking.

"How long do you know him?"

"Know him? Whom?"

"That man. Kassel."

"Who's Kassel?"

"Your Mannheim. Mannheim Incorporated. What you told me. You introduced us. How long?"

"What difference?"

"A Nazi. The worst. A Jew-killer. I thought I'd forgotten. God, like a nightmare."

"You're crazy."

"He is a part of what made me crazy."

"Mannheim. Konrad Mannheim. Not—Kassel. From Germany,

but he has been here many years, an established American. Anna, please, you are—are you?—still sick. Jew-killers. Here in America suddenly you see them again, Jew-killers?"

"He means something to you?"

"A year ago I worked for him; it is a year now. I was his secretary. I got a better job, more money, and I left. But a well-regarded man, a fine man, a distinguished man, an American business man. No, you must not say these things, you must not *see* these things."

"I saw! I tell you I *saw!* Gertrude, I know!"

"I beg of you. Doctors. There are doctors here, the best. I'll take you. . . ."

"I went."

"A doctor?"

"The consulate."

"Consulate!"

"Yesterday. To the Israeli consulate. I told them I had information. A Nazi murderer. A Jew-killer. Konrad Kassel."

"Did you tell them—Mannheim?"

"Kassel. Konrad Kassel."

"Did you say the name Mannheim?"

"Why do you keep asking that?"

"Why are you shouting, Anna? I'm asking. Did you say Mannheim?"

"No. I do not know a Mannheim. I know *him*. Kassel. SS Colonel Konrad Kassel. The man in the consulate was cold, severe. He did not help me. An official of the consulate—not one of the intelligence. He wrote down the few things he permitted me to say and promised me the intelligence, the people whose work it is, Shinbet of Israel. They will come."

"When?"

"Soon, he said. A few days. He was not happy with me, I know. I was another foolish woman taking up his time, another of the many who have ranted and chattered of Nazi war criminals over the long years. But they will come and I will tell them. Not of Mannheim—for that I will send them to you. I know nothing of your Mannheim. I know of SS Colonel Konrad Kassel, killer of Jews, murderer of his own father. I will tell of Kassel. You—*you* will tell of this Mannheim."

"Anna, dear God, you're crazy. I tell you you're crazy."

"I am not. Not!" And she was crying. Suppressing hysteria, hands clawed on her face, trembling, she collapsed on a couch.

She hated her. The strange sister, the crazy one. Whether or not this impossible story was the truth—she hated her. Some kind of insane jealousy? Had this strange one detected the tie between the younger spinster sister and the handsome man who had come to visit? Detestation of joy in the sibling? The need to destroy a suspected happiness in the younger one, always and by far the more beautiful? A part of the insanity?

Impossible, this sudden outburst, this crazy story. Konrad. Of all in the world—Konrad! But. Could it be? A lucidity? The sight of the man after all these years, his presence: had it accomplished the remembrance that five years of institutional probing had failed to accomplish? And if so, what? Even if. . . .

Those were other days, dead days, long ago, ancient. Mass murder, but most of the actual perpetrators were no more than soldiers under orders from a commander-in-chief who was a lunatic. Soldiers kill other soldiers in war; does each such death mark the other a murderer? Bombs kill civilians; is the bombardier a murderer or a soldier obeying orders in a campaign of war he himself does not understand? Anna was a sick woman, but suppose this *were* the truth? Then to hell with Anna and the truth. The past must not engulf the present; the very charges, the notoriety, could put an end to the nascent career he was so carefully planning, put an end to her own hope of happiness. And at that moment Gertrude Stryker was a murderer.

She was a murderer already, an accomplice in the plot to kill Lubeck, but this murder before Lubeck she must do herself and without Konrad ever knowing. She looked about for whisky, found nothing but the gin. She drank gin, comforted the sister, insisted they go out as they had planned for shopping. Anna washed, put on fresh makeup. They were ready. It was eleven o'clock.

She let Anna precede her and then there at the top of the stairway had struck out, pushed with all her strength at Anna's back, and Anna had toppled. All the way. A scream, a crash, and Anna lay limp and bleeding. The superintendent had rushed out from the downstairs apartment while she herself remained hidden behind the balustrade in the hallway on the first floor. Others had come out, neighbors, women, and she among them, all gathered about the still form; and then she had gone out to the street and to the car. And knew then what she would say if it went wrong: she herself had tripped and fallen against Anna. She drove home and was drunk the rest of that day.

She looked at her watch. Time now: soon he would be coming. She finished the drink, set down the glass, went to the bathroom, showered, combed her hair, and was perfuming her body when she heard his special ring. She ran nude to the door to greet her lover.

⚡ Thirteen

Petites Quiches au Jambon
Quenelles de Gibier
Cailles en Caisses a la Vigneronne
Consommé Chasseur
    Profiteroles
Cotelettes de Saumon aux Truffes à la Crême
    Concombres Etuves au Beurre
Noisettes de Veau à la Benevent
    Salade d'Endives
Souffle Ambassadrice
Fromages
Fruits
Cafe

Sherry 1821
Madeira 1884
Sainte-Croix-du-Mont 1921
Chateau-Lafite 1924

Gevrey-Chambertin 1929
Champagne 1934

TILLIE, in a green Valentina, was absolutely ravishing. For festive occasions she favored green, the color of her eyes, long narrow eyes, amused, sophisticated, cynical, but flecked with wrath this evening in clear disapprobation of his tardiness.

"Forgive me," he had said and she had nodded but continued talking with one of the guests and he had mingled with others, meekly admiring her from a distance.

She was exquisite in the Valentina gown, purchased as he knew (at a price that made him wince every time he thought of it) for this very gala. Green for her eyes and cut to reveal the figure of which she was justly proud. Tall tawny Tillie, a prattle of alliteration but somehow it summed her. Tall and tautly rounded in all the right places, all woman. And of a warm color: tan was the natural color of her skin. Many large teeth when she smiled, gleaming white teeth and gold-blonde hair and green eyes and tan skin and the only woman he had ever known who did not want to get married, really didn't (he was willing to foresake bachelorhood, and at his time in life)—that was his Tillie, only she wasn't very much his this evening. Once, before dinner, among the many people, when it happened he was alone with her, he said, "Aristotle."

"Yes?" The husky voice was not very encouraging. "Aristotle, Mr. McGregor?"

"What he said about beauty. 'The gift of God.'"

"Greek for Greek," she said. "Let me return a Greek to you, a couple of them, about beauty. Socrates—'A short-lived tyranny.' Theocritus—'An ivory mischief.' Well, this is one time you've roused the mischief in me, Mr. Maestro my co-host, an hour and a half late."

"Tillie, you're marvelous. You never fail to surprise."

"Why? Because I quote quotes right back at the master?" But she laughed. "I know. Coals to Newcastle."

But then they were divided again, surrounded within the conviviality of so many from all parts of the world gathered.

At the table, however, as host and hostess they were together, if not cheek by jowl then thigh by knee and in time Tillie thawed.

"What happened?"

"Business."

"Today? This day? Business?"

"I was certain it wouldn't encroach."

"But it did."

"Unexpected."

"How do you like the soup?"

"Extraordinary."

"My contribution, but your recipe. I insisted, and got a lot of respect from that damn mass of chefs in the kitchen. *Consommé Chasseur* with a few precious drops of that Sercial Madeira, vintage 1884."

"Tillie, I love you because you love to eat."

"That the best you can do about why you love me, Maestro?"

"I have other and better reasons but not for explication *en masse* at dinner."

"The *Consommé Chasseur.* Your recipe, which made them very respectful of me. And I insisted on all—the bones of venison, whole wild Mallard ducks, pheasants, partridges, Canadian hare. And for the *Quenelles de Gibier*—they are stuffed with the most delicate parts of the game we cooked in the soup. Could you have done better, Maestro?"

"I bow."

"Don't bow all the way, because on the *Noisettes de Veau à la Benevent,* a suggestion of the boys from outer space, they had me." The boys from outer space were three chefs especially flown in by the Confrerie des Chevaliers du Tastevin, three specially selected chefs from Paris. "Oh my, the turmoil in my kitchen, the clash of temperaments, but I admit on the *à la Benevent* I was ignorant. Now warmed by wonderful wine to the very cockles of my heart, I propose you a game, McGregor. I didn't know. Do you, Maestro? My game then. If you can tell me exactly what is *Noisettes de Veau à la Benevent* then you have won my forgiveness for having deserted me on your dastardly business for an hour and a half, leaving me all alone with all these lovely people."

Ah women. I love you all, women all over the world, I love womanliness.

"Do I have you, McGregor?"

"Reverse on that, my love. Literally. You made the game." He touched his napkin to his lips. "Let's see now. *Noisettes de Veau à la Benevent*. To begin—*veau*—calf, the young of the cow. The best of *veau* is the meat of calf aged from two to three months and fed exclusively on milk with some eggs added in the last few weeks. *Noisette* now, love. The *noisette* of veal is a rather fat part found in the shoulder to the left of the blade bone. In the middle of that part one can dig out a succulent, delicate little piece of meat no bigger than the size of a walnut and that, actually, is the *noisette*. And now *Noisettes à la Benevent*. Soak the *noisettes* over a tiny fire in lukewarm water for two hours, then blanch. Cool in cold water, drain, wipe. Then cook in a Madeira braising stock—having added diced carrots, diced onions, diced celery, a bit of belly of pork, thyme and bay leaf, all already sautéed in butter—and cook over a slow fire until tender. Serve garnished with a *macédoine de légumes au beurre* which is—"

"Enough. Enough! My God, McGregor, you're amazing."

"Thank you," he said and turned to talk to the man next to him but did not move his knee pleasantly juxtaposed to hers.

But as the dinner went on, she knew. McGregor valiantly trying. Courteous to all, polite, attentive, quick in the continuous conversation—but she knew. She felt his tension, his preoccupation.

"Bad?" she said.

"Pardon?"

"Today. The business."

"Not good."

"I'm sorry I was impatient."

"No. My fault."

And she talked to another, and he talked to another, and then she said, "Later? Will it be all right?"

"Yes, but I'll have to go away for a little time."

"When?"

"No specific hour. Later."

"For long?"

"No."

"You'll be able to come back?"

"Yes."

"I want you to. Please. We've so much to talk about. We've—

87

hardly. A crazy day, exciting. So much. But when you have to, tell me—I'll make the apologies."

"No, I can stay all the way through. No special time."

"How long?"

"Maybe an hour."

"And you'll come back to me?"

"I promise."

℞ Fourteen

HE was charming. A knowing, worldly, witty man, absolutely handsome; he had made a most wonderful evening for her. Once when she had started on business he had stopped her with, "No. What sense to rehash, Julie? We have an evening to enjoy, let's enjoy. There may not be many others. There may not be *any* others."

"You're right."

He had chosen a lovely restaurant, Barbetta, for dinner, and had chosen just the right kind of play, a frothy comedy. After the play he had not taken her to a supper club as she had half expected but to the Palm Court of the Plaza where there was light music and fragrant coffee and rich delicious French pastry. And not once during the evening a gauche move, no hint of the brashness of this afternoon; a wise, knowing man, a woman's man. She knew the game he was playing, it had been played with her before, but he played it so skillfully she was almost embarrassed to ask downstairs at the Delmonico, "Would you like a nightcap, Dave?"

"Love it."

"Tumblers from the toilet," she said. "I can't offer proper accouterments, this isn't my home. But the brandy as you know is excellent."

88

"Please. I'd love it."

And upstairs he helped her out of her wrap and she turned to him and took his face in her hands and kissed him. And then let him kiss her.

✌ Fifteen

McGREGOR and Tillie, alone. At two o'clock in Café Ulrich, McGregor and Tillie alone. At 2 A.M. the guests, the chefs, the waiters, the busboys, the sweepers, the dishwashers were all gone and the restaurant was clean and sparkling and ready for the morrow's business.

"Feel fresh as a daisy," Tillie said. "Crazy?"

"The excitement."

"I think I did it. Did I, Maestro?"

"Did you! They'll be talking about it all year. Perfect. Not a flaw."

"Praise from the master is praise indeed. One small favor, please, before you rush out into the night on your infernal affairs?"

"Yours always to command."

"Yeah," she said dryly. "Just this. A little walk, a little air. I'd go alone but I'm afraid. Would you be my guard, Inspector?"

"It would be my pleasure, Madame."

"I know I've been holding you."

"My pleasure when you hold me, Madame."

She closed up and they went out into the cool night air. They walked, came back. Café Ulrich on 60th Street near Madison Avenue was a two-story building, the entire upper floor Tillie's apartment. "I won't sleep. I couldn't possibly sleep," she said. "I'll be waiting."

"Yes," he said.

"I'm in the mood for a little drinking."

"Always best on a full stomach."

"How's your stomach, McGregor?"

"In the mood for a little drinking. Got something special up there?"

"Cuvee Royal Brut, '59. It'll be chilling. And if you disappoint me, I'll take a bottle in each hand and walk right out of a window."

"Not good out of a second-floor window. Sixteen stories is the absolute minimum for guaranteed effectiveness. Down to ten can do it, but no guarantee. Under that, splotch and botch."

"You ought to know, Mr. Homicide."

"A little sharp with me this evening, Miss Ulrich."

"I hate to let you go."

"I'll be back."

"Tell me again. When?"

"Within an hour."

"I'll be holding my breath."

"Hyperbole."

"Well, I'll be making myself beautiful."

"Making? You were *made* beautiful."

"McGregor, *once* can't you say the wrong thing?"

She kissed him quickly and went in.

He walked to Third Avenue, bought a *Times* already in a second morning edition, went into a cafeteria and ordered tea, took the tea and the *Times* to a table. He lit a cigarette and turned the many pages of the hefty *Times*. He did not find a report of a suicide but what he did find thankfully pre-empted an unpleasant piece of work and shortened the period before his return to Tillie.

It was on page 41 on the lower right-hand side nestled between the Mexican divorce of a jet-set married and a squib about burgeoning birth control clinics in India. It recited the facts of a death by apparent mugging, the body discovered behind the stairs in the rear of 218 Central Park South. The deceased was a male about forty years of age, unidentified, with a blond beard, an old scar over the right cheekbone, and a new wound, a bullet wound, in the right temple. The deceased had apparently met death resisting armed robbery; his clothes had been picked clean. He was not a tenant of the premises nor known to any of the tenants. Police were investigating, Detective-Lieutenant Louis Parker in charge. Anyone knowing anyone answering to the description of the deceased, call 440-1234.

Louis Parker, McGregor thought, an old-timer, an excellent policeman. It was unusual for the policeman in charge to have his name appear in the newspaper story which meant that Parker had made a point of requesting it, and McGregor understood. Parker was personally staying on top of it because Parker was unsatisfied and the reason was right there in the paper—"his clothes had been picked clean."

As McGregor knew, the bearded man had had the Luger, the key to apartment 4A, and thirty-nine dollars and sixty-seven cents. His visitor, upon discovering the body, was left with two choices—either calling the police and informing of the suicide he had found in the apartment, or divesting himself (or herself) of all connection with the corpse—and quite obviously he had undertaken the second course. To accomplish the desired effect he had had to appropriate the Luger and the key to the apartment and the money and that had left a cadaver as cleanly plucked of personal property as a chicken of feathers before cooking.

Mugger is modern lingo for highway thief and a thief takes valuables, he does not strip the clothes of his victim of every blessed item of belongings, and Detective-Lieutenant Louis Parker was wise, bright, experienced. This was no routine mugging and he was not routinely dismissing it as another death during the commission of robbery; he was keeping it open and keeping his hand in.

McGregor lit a cigarette, folded away the newspaper. All evening the valise in the corner of his bedroom had been nagging at a corner of his mind, and now there was time. At least for a quick look. He paid, went out, and got a cab.

The leather glowed with age. It was thick, wide, heavy, and old-fashioned with two sturdy straps, held firmly in leather slots, tightly buckled about it, and two huge, fluted, decorative snap-locks neither of which had a hole for a key. It was a beautiful piece of luggage, foreign, well-crafted, old but in excellent condition. He had to sit on it in order to loosen the strain on the straps so he could open the buckles, then he snapped the locks and the cover sprang open and he continued to sit, on the floor, as he examined the contents.

Two suits. Two shirts. Two undershirts. Two pairs of shorts. One tie. Two pairs of socks. One pair of shoes. One pair of pajamas. One pair of house slippers. A bathrobe. A comb, a brush, an electric shaver. (Just enough to get by on. He had either come for a short visit or he had planned to enlarge his wardrobe. Electric shaver? Well, one has to trim one's beard.) But beneath all of that there was finally material of interest.

A passport: he was Ludwig Lubeck from Buenos Aires, Argentina. A tiny envelope that contained a key: a bank vault key, unquestionably, there are no other keys quite like them. A regular-size envelope that contained $11,000 in American money. Another regular-size envelope, this one heavily sealed with tape. It bore an inscription that he recognized as German and it did not require a masterpiece of deduction to conclude that whatever was written inside was also written in German. He put this envelope aside. The last was also an envelope, slit open, postmarked three weeks ago and addressed in a bold hand to Ludwig Lubeck, the return address: Konrad Mannheim, 218 Central Park South, New York, N.Y. U.S.A. Inside, a note in the same bold handwriting. *Dear Ludwig, I am in receipt of your recent letter for which I thank you. We shall of course be in telephone conversation before you come permanently to New York. Sincerely, Konrad Mannheim.* And so McGregor had another insight into Mr. Mannheim. A shrewd apple. Didn't commit himself in writing. Concise and conservative.

He repacked the bag with all but the sealed envelope, stood up from the floor and decided, as long as he was home, to change from his dinner clothes. Then he took up the envelope and grinned. He had a date with the translator. German was Tillie Ulrich's mother tongue.

When she opened the door for him he knew immediately that the time for translation was not now. The lights were sultry and so was Tillie in green, formfitting hostess pajamas.

"Well done, McGregor."

"What?" he demanded.

"You've returned to heart and hearth well within the hour."

"Oh."

"You like?" She lifted her arms, pirouetted.

Somehow she was going too fast for him, his mind was involved in other matters. "You've been at the champagne, my love, haven't you?"

"But have I. Bottle's in the cooler in the kitchen. Well, do you like?"

"You I like. Love."

"The garment. Of purest silk serene. An indoors pants-suit. Adorable? A Valentina creation. But you must be sheer underneath, absolutely, indecently, deliciously naked."

He moaned, laughed. " 'To paint the lily.' And at those prices!"

"I have two more—creations, and I'm dying to show you. Get comfortable. I'll model them. Yes?"

"Yes."

"Drink, McGregor. You can use it."

"It shows?"

"Your enthusiasm. Devastating."

"I'm enthusiastic," he grumbled and went for the champagne in the kitchen.

> To gild refined gold, to paint the lily,
> To throw a perfume on the violet,
> To smooth the ice, or add another hue
> Unto the rainbow, or with taper-light
> To seek the beauteous eye of heaven to garnish,
> Is wasteful and ridiculous excess.

✌ Sixteen

LATER, much later, he showed her the envelope.

"Ho? So? What?" She kissed him. "What's this?"

"What's it say there in German?"

She translated easily. *To Be Opened Only in the Event of My Violent Death. Otherwise To Be Destroyed Without Opening.* And looked up at him. "You were given this for safekeeping?"

"No. Open it."

"But it says—"

"You just told me."

"But—"

"Violent death. He's dead. Violently. Open it, please."

She used a nail file to slit open the envelope, extracted and unfolded a long sheet of paper closely written.

"German," she said.

"Naturally. Now read for me, please. But slowly."

It is my hope that no one will ever read this missive. It is my hope that I myself, in time, shall destroy it. But until that time when at last I know assuredly I am safe, until then I live in fear of the very one closest to me because he alone knows, and knowing he also knows (and I know) that my death can doubly enrich him. It is therefore I have penned this missive. If I live and all goes as planned, I shall destroy it. If he kills me, by however clever his method—and he is the cleverest man I know—then I have left behind this writing which will be my posthumous vengeance. Yes, I fear. He is the cleverest of men, which is why I chose him. But cleverness cuts two ways. In his own protection, rather than for the additional riches, he may desire me dead because alive I can implicate him. True, to implicate him I myself must be implicated—but one must reckon with exceeding cleverness. Alive, my very existence—my being—is a threat to him. Dead, the threat is forever removed and he is also doubly enriched financially. It is because I can understand his temptation that I am writing this missive. I hope I am wrong. I hope years will pass and I can then destroy this letter as the work of a small, mean, suspicious, contemptible individual, all of which I admit I am. In all truth, he has been quiet, kind, understanding, cooperative, albeit acquisitive, and not by one single word or deed can he be charged or suspected. Any suspicion, fear, fright, reflection on his character is I admit within me and without any given cause on his part. And now to me. And to cause and effect.

I am a thief. I am a weak thief, the worst kind, but it was that very weakness, my flabbiness—not my body which is strong and powerful, not my brain which is sharp and acute, but my soul, my personality, which is without push, thrust, without daring—that placed me, all over the long years, in a position of monstrous temptation. Who would think I would dare?

In Buenos Aires I was a bookkeeper, and a good one, and as a member of the National Socialist League of Argentina I rose steadily until at a rather young age I was established in the permanent, and enviable position for one of my years, of treasurer.

I am not a politician, not politically inclined, have no political interest or ambition. What I mean to say is that I am not a zealot, have no burning allegiance to the League.

I was completely trusted. Of course they did not think I would dare tamper. I handled all the money. I had office assistants, but they were people whom I hired to help me, secretaries and clerical workers, minor people. I was in charge of all money matters. I handled the books.

People outside our affairs cannot possibly know of the enormous amounts of money that pour from all over the world into the League week after week, month after month, year after year—from wills, trusts, estates, individual gifts and philanthropic donations. Despite its vast expenditures in every civilized country, the League at certain periods would have a surplus in excess of $100,000,000 in its treasury. Needless to say it was not difficult to pilfer comparatively small amounts, and $100,000 a year was small in that vast financial network; the books were mine to keep balanced and that was easily done.

When years ago I grew a beard they laughed at me and joked about my vanity. It was not vanity, it was part of my gradual, long-time plan, a ten-year plan. And during that period I remained alone, with no close friends. I did not marry. The wife of my youth, a slut, I divorced as a youth. For ten long years I was consecrated to a plan, but when my time finally came I was too frightened to know what to do. I had the money, hidden in separate portions in various unlikely places, not in banks or bank vaults; I did not wish to rouse any possible suspicion by being seen near or connected with financial institutions except on business for the League. I was weak, frightened. My time had come, but I needed help.

Mannheim. Exactly the opposite of me. Strong, resolute, fearless, powerful. A man from whom, like a parasite, I could suck the strength I needed to sustain me. During his visits in Buenos Aires, I cultivated him, toadied him, sounded him out, became resolved that he was my man, confessed and made him my offer.

With one such as Mannheim you do not seek his seduction by the bait of a small bribe. My first offer was my full offer—one-half of my ten-year accumulation in return for his brain, his wit, his alliance and aid in the final consummation. He brilliantly questioned me, learned all, my methods, procedures, protections, and my plans and dreams for the future, and acquiesced and became my accomplice post facto and my partner in the last stages of the long embezzlement.

It is necessary to inform of Mannheim. Konrad Mannheim is the name in America. The true name is Konrad von Kassel, of long and ancient and honorable lineage in the Fatherland. Konrad Mannheim, president of Mannheim Incorporated, 277 Park Avenue, City of New York, State of New York, U.S.A. Residence apartment 4A, 218 Central Park South,

City of New York, State of New York, U.S.A. Unmarried. Keeps a mistress, Gertrude Stryker, in apartment 3D, 58 Beverly Road in the province of Flushing, Borough of Queens, City of New York, State of New York, U.S.A.

Mannheim is the new anointed. He closes his affairs in America. He returns to the new Germany, a figure prepared for political welcome and prestige. All quiet, all beneath, all political subterranean. In Germany the *Blau Gruppe* has tilled fertile soil for the fresh growing of the new anointed, and from Buenos Aires the League has spilled forth huge monies for the flowering of the enterprise.

I believe I have chosen well. I am linked with the anointed. He has advised and I have listened. We are partners, we are pals, each understands the other.

With him I have had strength. My directions became chartered within his direction. On my trips up to the States I brought installments of the money. He took a vault in his name, Konrad Mannheim, in the Lincoln National Bank, 44 Street and Madison Avenue, City of New York, State of New York, U.S.A. But he gave me the key—just as he gave me a key to his apartment. The vault in his name, but the key in my possession. A gesture, but in fact a noble gesture. If he would wish to bilk me, there cannot be a contest. I am no match for him, I do not pretend to be. But this much I know—to bilk me he must in the end kill me, and it is therefore I am putting pen to this missive.

Now, under his advice I have resigned my position with the League. I come to America where Mannheim will quietly install me in a hotel until we leave—with the money—for Germany. I am much more calm now. I have a leader, an advisor, a man of action who will make reality out of my plans and dreams.

In Buenos Aires they may never discover the well-covered irregularities; the books are well balanced, and I must state with a certain pride that the peculations were done with such skill and woven within the affairs of the League in such complex manner as to be virtually undiscoverable. If by some remote incident of chance such discovery is made, I shall be by then far away and safe.

In Germany I shall shave off the beard so long worn, which immediately makes one another man. Then there will be a change of name, and Mannheim will procure all new papers for me. He can do it. He has power and authority in the Fatherland. Then—and this was his suggestion and a good one—he will arrange for a plastic surgeon to remove the scar on my right cheek.

And so, reborn, I shall proceed with plan and dream. Independently wealthy, I shall purchase a small farm in Bavaria, marry a peasant girl, have a family, and live out my life in peace and contentment. In essence, I am just that—a dreamer and a man of peace, perhaps even somewhat of a fool. I have no strength of nature, no force of ambition, no brilliant brain. Mannheim provides what I lack.

I hope and pray this confession will never be read. I hope and pray there will not be the need. I shall carry through with my end of our agreement. If Mannheim carries through with his, then once I am settled and safe this missive will be, gratefully, destroyed.

Ludwig Lubeck

℞ Seventeen

"WHEW!" Tillie folded the paper, inserted it in the envelope. "Quite a—'missive.' Something, Maestro?"

McGregor was silent.

"Do you think it's for real?" Tillie asked.

"I propose to find out."

"A million dollar robbery. And the man doesn't think *they'll* ever find out."

"Not robbery. Embezzlement."

"Can it happen? I mean that it's never found out?"

"Not robbery which by definition means the taking by force or intimation."

She made a face. "All right, all right, you and your technicalities. Embezzlement."

"Yes it can happen."

"Got you, McGregor." She laughed. "If there's an embezzlement that was never found out—how would you know there was an embezzlement?"

"Process of reasoning. Logic. Embezzlement is usually a slow, secret appropriation of money by a person in a position to be entrusted with such money. There have been gigantic embezzlements that were discovered years and years later—twenty years or more—sometimes only at the death of the embezzler. Stands to reason that there must be embezzlements that remain forever undiscovered depending upon the type of business, the type of supervision, the state of affairs of the business, and the sagacity of the perpetrator. If you're in a position to embezzle, you're also in a position to cover up. *Quid pro quo.*"

"So much for the Latin, lover. Why so dour?"

"Me dour?"

"Need a crowbar to pry a smile out of you. Do you think this Mannheim killed him?" She reached over, put cool fingers to his lips, and closed his mouth that had opened round. She tapped the envelope. *"To Be Opened Only in the Event of My Violent Death. Otherwise To Be Destroyed Without Opening.* You yourself told me he was dead by violence. His 'missive' tells us he feared Mannheim. So why so agape when I ask if you think Mannheim killed him?"

"Tillie, at the risk of boring you with the repetition—you're marvelous."

"You mean I hit it? Mannheim killed him?"

"You didn't hit it which doesn't make you not marvelous."

"He *is* dead?"

"Yes." He took the envelope from her.

"And by violence?"

"Yes."

"Oh. Could be accident. I mean a violent accident could be violence."

"No, he was killed."

99

"And Mannheim didn't kill him?"

"Not Mannheim."

"Do you know who?"

"Yes."

"Can you tell me?"

"I want to."

"Who?"

"I."

There was silence.

Then there was movement.

Then they were each in another room, he in the living room and she in the kitchen making coffee. And then with coffee and cigarettes in the living room, he said, "I'm going to tell you a bit of this because I'm going to need you. It'll also explain why I was late for dinner and why I had to leave you after the dinner. We'll begin with Mannheim. Seems he's disappeared. I have a client who retained me to find him. . . ."

And when he was finished she shivered. "God, and it's supposed to be a glamorous racket you're in."

He sipped coffee. "Now from the 'missive' I've got some live leads to work with."

"You think it was Mannheim who lugged him out and put him under the stairs?"

"Could be but needn't be. Remember my client's pretty much a liar and I don't know who she is really, and what in hell she's up to."

"Nice looking?"

"Pardon?"

"The client. Pretty?"

"Don't go feminine on me."

"Would you prefer me masculine?"

He got up, went to the phone, dialed a number, and a voice answered on the first ring.

"Police. Homicide. Yes?"

"Detective-Lieutenant Louis Parker, please."

"Not in. Something I can do for you?"

"When is he due?"

"Who is this?"

"McGregor."

"Who?"

"Ex-Inspector McGregor."

Alertly now. "Oh. Hi, Inspector."

"Hi. When's he due?"

"Eight o'clock. Eight to four, his action this shift. But you know Parker. Comes before and never leaves."

"Would you put down a message for him, please?"

"Pleasure."

"Tell him I'll be in to see him at eight o'clock sharp."

"Right, Inspector."

"Thank you."

"Thank *you*, Inspector."

He hung up.

Tillie said: "You turning yourself in?" No reaction. His eyes were far away. "Maestro!"

"Huh?"

"You turning yourself in?"

"Ha, ha," he dutifully laughed but without risibility. "Tillie, could you be at my place tomorrow noon?"

"Is that an order, Boss?"

"Can you make it?"

"For how long? I run a restaurant; remember me?"

"Couple of hours, maybe less."

"If you want me."

"I always do."

"No!" But she had to laugh. My McGregor. Preoccupied or no, eyes far away or not, he never fails to come up with a pleasing answer. "I mean if you want me tomorrow noon. No, no! Maestro, you're confusing me."

"I want you now."

"Tomorrow noon, my gallant. Okay, date, your apartment, tomorrow noon, and from the look of you it's something special. Is it?"

"I think so."

"Like what, special?"

"We're going to rob a bank."

℞ Eighteen

DETECTIVE-Lieutenant Louis Parker, carrying a cardboard container of coffee, came into his office at a quarter to eight, looked over the duty board, looked over his messages, smiled when he saw the message from McGregor, entered his inner office and closed the door. He made several quick necessary phone calls, then removed the top of the container and enjoyed the coffee. Routine: breakfast at home, then the second coffee here before the first cigar of the day. And smiled again, thinking of McGregor, already a legend in the Department. And grunted. Inspector McGregor, living legend. But by damn the man *was* a legend, a legendary figure, and he of all people, Louis Parker, hard as rock and about as easily impressed—Louis Parker ought to know and he damn did know. Christ, the guy was my boss for twenty long years. And smiled, thinking of times past working with McGregor, and lit a cigar.

What made McGregor McGregor? Dichotomy. Dichotomy upon dichotomy, splinter within splinter, ramification, divergence, numerousness, many men within one—that made McGregor McGregor. A poet as a policeman? Ridiculous. But this poet had been as tough a cop as there was in the business, never once, however, breaching law. It was McGregor who had preached all over the years what the Supreme Court had finally burnished as law—but what had always been the law—that a person in the hands of police should not be questioned before first being informed of his constitutional rights; that he had a right to say nothing, that whatever he did say could be held against him, and that he had an immediate right to an attorney. Yet McGregor had established a record, never yet broken, for having elicited more confessions than any other man in the Department. McGregor the non-conformist, the unpredictable. Slow, easy, learned, professorial, he was nonetheless a belt-man in karate. A darling of the academicians who used to beg for his appearance on their lecture platforms, he was nonetheless feared and respected by the roughest of the professional criminals. A man of remarkable, uncanny memory—he could spot and identify a face he had seen a generation ago—he would forget daily trivialities and an aide would have to remind him of such things as a date with the Governor, or a dinner in Washington being given in his honor by the Department of Justice. Not a stereotype but the best damn policeman in the Department, a career man, he had nonetheless retired immediately upon the expiration of his twenty-year service, despite the offer of the top job. That had been a time of change in the municipal administration and the new mayor had unequivocally offered him the commissionership and McGregor had unequivocally turned it down. The reason? Parker, among other dignitaries, had heard him. "I want to sleep, Mr. Mayor. A man like me in my job I haven't had sleep, a real sleep, a sleep without worry of awakening, in twenty years, and for twenty years I've been dreaming of the time when I could sleep as long as I want whenever I want, and now for me my time has come and I'm young enough. Over the years I've made a few investments, and now the pension, and I'll get me a card from Albany to operate as a private detective, but operate when and if I please. I've put in my time, *all* of my time, for twenty years. I've set up rules, standards, regulations, even personal example; now my time has come to sleep whenever I want to sleep; each man to his own; there is other work. I thank you, Mr. Mayor. I am honored. I decline."

Now McGregor was coming early in the morning so it figured to be important—at least for McGregor—but no complaint. With McGregor, whatever it was, it would be stimulating and refreshing. And promptly at eight o'clock—Parker checked his watch —there was a knock and a policeman put his head in and said, "Inspector McGregor."

"Sure," Parker said.

McGregor was smiling but rumpled and sat down immediately.

Parker, who had been standing, sat.

And put new fire to his cigar.

"Inspector, a pleasure."

"How are you, Louie?"

"Fine. You?"

"Fine. How's business?"

Parker chewed his cigar. "Never lets up. They keep killing each other."

> " 'Yet each man kills the thing he loves,
>   By each let this be heard,
> Some do it with a bitter look,
>   Some with a flattering word,
> The coward does it with a kiss,
>   The brave man with a sword.' "

"You come to Homicide at eight o'clock in the morning in order to recite Oscar Wilde?"

McGregor applauded. "You're an educated man, Louie."

"Sort of force-fed. For twenty years I worked under a professor-type."

"Deprecation, sheer deprecation. Happens there's much I learned from *you*."

"Not about Oscar Wilde. Not one of my favorite people. A wiseacre-type artist, too brittle, too polished-shiny, too superficial for the likes of me."

" 'Each man kills the thing he loves.' That guy killed himself; not suicide but he sure did. Dead at forty-four. Death wish. Just shook the house until the ceiling fell in on him. Yes, brittle, polished-shiny, but there's always another side. Death again, as long as here we are at Homicide. Sort of an epitaph.

> 'Tread lightly, she is near
>   Under the snow,
> Speak gently, she can hear
>   The daisies grow.'

Quite soft, sweet, tender. Wouldn't think that was Wilde, would you?"

"Inspector, *did* you come to discuss Oscar Wilde?"

"I came for a little horse trading, Louie."

Parker grinned. "You need a favor, Inspector?"

"Yes. And so do you, Lieutenant."

"Me?"

"About a fella got found dead. An alleged mugging victim. Two-eighteen Central Park South." McGregor's turn to grin. "I notice they put you in the papers as the policeman."

Parker grunted, got up, walked, his heels noisy. He stopped behind McGregor who did not turn around and the tableau suddenly embarrassed him because he had learned the gambit from the very man on whom he was pulling it. "When your pants are at half mast," the inspector had lectured long ago, "don't let your pigeon notice. Get behind him and talk from behind him until you've collected yourself."

"Put me in the papers as the policeman," Parker said. "Not a mugging. Figures murder made to look like mugging. The guy was stripped clean, nothing left, nothing even for identification. We got him on ice. Figures quick enough somebody'll be calling him in as a Missing Person. At least we'll know whom the hell we got."

"There won't be a call."

"*Somebody* will miss him."

"Nobody."

"How the hell you know?"

"I know. Come out from behind, Louie. Stop hiding."

Parker paced. Heels noisy. Embarrassedly. All around McGregor. Then he sat down behind his desk, but facing McGregor, and put new fire to his cigar. "What's up?"

"A little horse trading."

"What do you know about my guy?"

"I know who he is, where he's from, and who killed him."

"You know—*how?*"

"It's tied in with a thing I'm working on."

"When does it get untied?"

McGregor shrugged. "I don't know. But when it does, you'll have your full story on the fellow with the beard. Not a mugging; you're one hundred percent correct. Actually he wasn't murdered, in the precise sense of the word. He was killed in self-defense. I

105

believe he was set up to be murdered—but before the murderer, the intended murderer, arrived—there was an intervention. Motive—money."

"You mean the guy who intervened?"

"No. The guy who intended the murder. An old equation in our business—two minus one equals one. A couple of guys involved in an enormous heist. The heist worked, and so Step One was accomplished, but you're in the racket, Lieutenant, and you know the kind of trouble that can happen between Step One and Step Two."

"Step Two being two parts—division of spoils and then the scattering of the co-workers."

"Correct. In this case, only two co-workers. And so we come to the epigram that has been the delight of police since time immemorial—that there is honor among thieves, a grievous misstatement of fact. Hell, if you're a thief *already* you're without honor." McGregor lit a cigarette. "Chesterton put it prettily and wittily: 'Thieves respect property. They merely wish the property to become their property that they may more perfectly respect it.' "

"And so out of respect, one of your two thieves planned the murder of the other and like that the property achieves its pinnacle of respectability."

"Excellent, Louie. More, the remaining thief doubles his share of the property and halves the possibility of culpable involvement. Two can keep a secret only if one is dead." And now McGregor, out of the chair, was walking. "I think I've got it shaped, Lieutenant, but it's got a little bug and that's biting me. Which is the reason I'm asking for trade. If you can clear the bug, we've got our case."

"Mr. McGregor, you've told me nothing; I hope you realize that. I mean I hope you realize that I realize it."

"I realize that you realize that I realize that I've pulled you in for a horse trade. How're we doing, Louie?"

Parker laid away his cigar.

"Just what, please, do you wish of me?"

McGregor chuckled. "There. You see? Cooperation. That's all I've come for, all I'm asking, a bit of cooperation."

"Like," Parker growled, "what?"

"The little bug in my ratiocinations, a lovely fly in my sticky ointment."

"Like," Parker growled, "who?"

"A beautiful lady."

"*Who?*"

"That's what I'm about to ask of you. To find out for me. Who. The bug that needs the clearing. If she's mixed in this, I can be all wet. If she's not, I'm dry. Her name, at least the name I know—Juliette Gaza. Address—Delmonico Hotel, Suite Fourteen Hundred. I'm not to be mentioned."

"Cooperation." Parker snorted. "What you're asking—that I lock her up, put the screws to her. And you're the guy that's always preached law. It's false arrest."

"I'm not asking that."

"Not much. We trump up a charge, bring her in, scare her shitless, squeeze her for information before she gets her wits about her and then—"

"Hold it!" McGregor stubbed out his cigarette. "Not at all that drastic, Louie, and nothing illegal. What's required here is a bit of intimidation. You go up there, you and a couple of uniformed policemen. Sure you scare her; but no improper search and seizure, nothing like that. But you threaten, you know? You've had a tip that she's—some international jewel thief. Make up a name. Same initials, that always puts a fillip on it. Jane Grant." He smiled. "International jewel thief, real melodramatic. Look, you know what I want and you know how to handle it. Stop playing games."

Parker took up his cigar, flicked off the lifeless ash, bit down on the wet stump, and talked through his teeth.

"Then what?"

"Pump. Get all you can. And if possible, verify."

"Then?"

"Back with me. We're horse trading."

"If I deliver—when do you deliver?"

"I can't give you a time, Louie. It doesn't figure for long, in my opinion. A guy's dead, and there's a lot of loot lying around. If I'm thinking right—and if you clear my bug I *am* thinking right —then the other guy's not going to put in for long delays. Keep your file open, but don't waste any more time with it. I've still got

107

work in front of me, but I promise you a full solution. Now will you please get moving on the lady Gaza?"

Parker looked over his calendar. "First chance—I can give it a try at about eleven."

"Fine. Try."

"Where'll I be able to reach you?"

"After eleven—home. Will you be in touch, however you make out?"

"You'll hear from me, Inspector."

"Thank you, Lieutenant."

℘ Nineteen

McGREGOR rode in a taxi to his garage and there the garageman, beaming, said as though it were an event, "Well, it's so good to see you, sir." In a way it was an event and they saw one another rarely because McGregor rarely used his car. In the City of New York, the city of taxis (except when it's raining), who needs a car? He hated driving; it was no longer a sport as it had been in his youth. For long trips he was driven: he would hire a car and chauffeur. But for the shorter trips, to outlying districts of the city proper, it was necessary. The law specifically stated that a taxi must take you anywhere in the metropolitan area but it was a law as flouted as a law against adultery. So to outlying districts he drove, grudgingly. Outlying districts were no part of the McGregor rote, and so his visits to the garage were infrequent. "Good to see you, how are you?" he said. "May I have Bluebird?"

"Yessir, indeed. Just you stay where you are. I'll bring her right down."

Bluebird was vintage but in excellent condition and it purred without cough or jolt through the exhaust fumes and the air pollution. It was not until he was quit of the Manhattan traffic that McGregor was able to admire the bright and shiny morning about him. He rolled down all the windows, let the breeze stir through the car as it whipped along the highway. Once out of Manhattan, the traffic eased and the pace was swift. He arrived at Beverly Road thirty-five minutes after leaving the garage, drove past No. 58, parked a block away, and walked back along a tree-lined street.

The house was tall, wide, old, its brick ivy-covered, its lobby spacious, a bank of self-service elevators in the rear. He entered one, touched the 3-button, emerged into a broad, well-lighted hallway.

Three-D had a neatly embossed nameplate, white on black in a burnished brass bracket: STRYKER. He pushed the doorbell, got no answer, pushed again, no answer, shook his head, tried the knob in a futile reactive gesture—and it turned.

The doorknob turned.

He entered into a tiny foyer. "Hello?"

All quiet. The closing of the door was a large noise, and then in the silence he called again, softly, "Hello?" And walked, without knowing why, on tiptoe, into an immaculate apartment, calling: "Hello? Hello?"

No echo. No answer. Silence.

He was in a living room, well furnished, all in order except for the incongruity of a single glass on a coaster at a corner of a table. He went near. The glass was empty save for a slice of lemon peel, brown, dry. He put his nose to the mouth of the glass, sniffed. Nothing. All odor had evaporated. He straightened, stiff against a shiver of portent. He was an old cop. Something was wrong.

First thought upon finding the doorlock snapped open was that she had gone out—to the superintendent, or to a neighbor for a moment, and having mislaid her keys had left the door unlocked. Quite within reason, not unusual. But the glass. A bad fit. It didn't belong. Not in a room so right, so perfectly in order, fastidiously arranged. Not a glass recently drunk from and momentarily set away. Obviously it had been a highball, but old: the odor dissipated, the lemon peel discolored and shriveled. Who cleans that well, but forgets a highball glass with its residue of peel? Had she been interrupted? When?

He moved quickly now.

The bedroom like the living room in perfect order. This early in the morning the bed was made, but the shades were drawn. He looked in the closets. Good clothes, all neatly hung; and now here on a side table by the bed, a handbag. He sought and found— keys. (So? Why an open door?) For the rest the handbag contained the usual feminine articles—lipstick, compact, tissues— and a wallet with a driver's license, a social security card, and $162 in cash.

He inspected neatly stacked drawers, found nothing that linked her with Mannheim or Lubeck. He found three savings bankbooks showing a sum total of $27,850.23. He found letters from a sister, Anna, who was coming from Australia to the United States en route to Israel.

The bathroom was different. Although clean, there was disarray. The door of a stall-shower was open. Outside the shower, a bath mat lay on the tiled floor. He touched it. Dry. Two used towels hung from a rack. He touched them. Dry. A comb, lying along the edge of the sink, had hair in it.

He went out of the bathroom and through the bedroom and living room to the kitchen. Spotless. All in order. Except for three aluminum grates that were neatly stacked on the kitchen counter. For a moment they puzzled him, unfamiliar but somehow familiar, and then he knew why. One rarely sees them out of position and one takes them for granted in position. They were the removable, horizontal grates that created the partitions of a refrigerator.

He turned to the refrigerator, tall, white, but suddenly ominous.

He pulled open the door and the nude body tumbled out.

℞ Twenty

SHE was a small woman and even in death a beautiful woman. The tiny bullet hole was hardly a mar. Directly in the center of her forehead, it looked somehow like the decorative mark on an Eastern woman. A .22 he guessed, and any bleeding had been internal. Squatting, he examined the back of her head. No wound. The bullet had not smashed through, a break for the ballistics people. He stood up and looked in the refrigerator. Empty. He went out of the kitchen and out of the apartment into the hallway, and saw the incinerator nearby. An easy job to clean out the refrigerator and dump the contents. He went back to the kitchen and replaced the body.

He paced through the apartment, touching nothing now, a cop working. An inside job but not a professional job; an inside job with an attempt to make it look like an outside job by the simple expedient of leaving the snap-lock open. Like that it *could* be a stranger, an intruder. There are sneak-operators who every day in the week and every hour in the day, somewhere in the city, are trying doors. Especially the doors of women living alone. Purpose: thievery, or rape, or both. But there had been no thievery here: the wallet in the handbag contained $162. Sexual molestation? It was possible that autopsy would determine there *had* been sexual molestation, but from the physical evidence he doubted it. There was no sign whatever of a struggle. True she was nude, but then where were the clothes? Would a rape-artist after stripping her, carefully hang away her clothes in the bedroom closet? And would he, after murdering her so that she could never identify him, remove the contents of the refrigerator to the incinerator, and stuff her in; a body in an icebox?

He sat in a chair in the living room, and sitting he was working. Let's reconstruct here; not too tough, this has been my business all my life. Let's start with the door. As she was a woman alone, it had probably been locked before the murder and unlocked *after* the murder by the murderer; his attempt at a red herring. So far, so good. He looked about. A sparkling clean apartment, all in order, except for the glass here in the living room. Fine. While she had been cleaning, she had been drinking. Then, finished cleaning, she had left the glass either for more drink later or to put the glass away later, and had gone for a shower. From living room to bedroom to bathroom contiguous to bedroom. In the bedroom she had hung away whatever clothes she had been wearing before stepping into the bathroom. In the bathroom quite evidently she had showered but there had been no opportunity to clean up the bathroom: witness the open door of the stall-shower, the bath mat on the floor, the used towels hanging crumpled from the rack. She was combing her hair—witness comb with hair on sink—when someone had rung the bell and she had run to answer it. Why not? It fit. But what woman runs from her bathroom to answer her doorbell without first putting on a robe, something? Answer: a beautiful woman, proud of her body, running to answer the ring of an expected lover. It fit. It damn fit. From Lubeck's letter we know she had a lover with motive for murder, a million dollar's worth of motive. Who but a mistress is kin to the lover's knavery? But a knave intent upon full clearance from crime will cut off from himself both accomplice and mistress. It fit. And the body in the icebox, that fit too. Refrigeration. No stink of putrefaction. Time. Time to be away, gone, cut off from events here in the States, and according to Lubeck's missive Mannheim's permanent departure to Europe was imminent. *He closes his affairs in America. He returns to the new Germany.* Well, if I'm right he sure closed *this* affair in America with a bang. Two bangs. A bang in the head and a bang of the refrigerator door. Could be I'm wrong, but if I'm right Mr. Konrad Mannheim sure has been having himself a busy time. McGregor sighed, slapped his knees, stood up, and went out, and downstairs he walked in dappled sunshine under trees with green leaves.

He drove a short distance, stopped at a phone booth. He inserted a coin, dialed a number, said, "Hello? Police? This is an innocent bystander."

"What? Whatsat?"

"Innocent bystander. I wish to report a murder. Have them go up and look, please. Fifty-eight Beverly Road. Apartment 3D. Thank you. Bye now."

And hung up.

And lit a cigarette.

And got back in the car.

And drove home thinking all the way, quite seriously, about taking on a wife, except he realized that his was a unique situation. He was in love and knew she was in love but as reluctant as he had been all his life he knew she was even more reluctant. The lovely Tillie was the only woman he had ever known who when she said she did not want to get married *meant* it. And she said she did not want to get married. Now how do you like *them* apples, Mr. McGregor?

> Wives are young men's mistresses,
> companions for middle age,
> and old men's nurses.

℘ Twenty-one

A LATE morning, a late breakfast. The dishes were still there on the breakfast trays as she yawned, stretched, and admired the reflection in the pier mirror. Chic, the lounging pajamas. Ah, Paree. Perfectly decent, the soft white silk lounging pajamas purchased in Paris, but somehow indecent. *Tres chic.* And laughed at herself in the mirror, and fluffed at her hair, and the bell rang.

A frown. She looked at her watch. 11:30. He was only just gone. Five minutes ago. Promising to be back at three. Had he left something? Or was it Room Service for the breakfast dishes?

She went quickly, opened the door, and her hand became a fist on the knob.

A thick dark man with authoritative eyes, and behind him two tall uniformed policemen.

"Miss Grant?"

"I beg your pardon?"

"Jane Grant?"

"Who is Jane Grant?"

"You."

"Some mistake. I am Juliette Gaza."

"No mistake, Miss Grant."

He pushed in, the policemen behind him, and the door slammed. "Parker," he said. "Lieutenant Parker." He flipped out his wallet. On one side was the gold badge, and on the other, protected by transparent plastic, his official card: LOUIS PARKER, NEW YORK CITY POLICE DEPARTMENT. He put away the wallet, showed tobacco-stained teeth in a grim smile.

"Okay, Miss Grant, get dressed."

"Dressed? I *am* dressed, Mr. Parker."

"Okay if that's the way you want it, Miss Grant."

"I am *not* Miss Grant and I *am* dressed."

"Okay if that's the way you want us to take you downtown, Miss Grant."

"Downtown? What's downtown?"

"A colloquialism, Miss Grant. The formal place for interrogation."

"Now look here, mister. I am not Grant, Jane Grant. I am trying to be calm. You've made a mistake; I assure you—you've made some kind of terrible mistake. Now look. If you please. Before you get yourself into trouble with your own officialdom may I identify myself?"

"Please."

She left them and came back with her passport, displayed it. "Juliette Gaza. From West Germany. I only came here yesterday. Somewhere you've gone wrong, Mr. Parker. I'm not Jane Grant; I've never heard of a Jane Grant."

He studied the passport, returned it to her.

"Maybe you're Gaza. Maybe you're Grant. That's why I'm here. Now let me give it to you plain, honey. Jane Grant—which is only one of her many names—Jane Grant is a sharp little cookie; the police of five countries have been trying to come up against Jane Grant. Now don't give me that put-upon look, honey, that offended glare; it's been given to me before in my life and it doesn't cut the mustard. Now just listen. Jane Grant is the front for an international group of wise operators dealing in hot stones; Jane Grant brings in the stones and peddles them. We got a tip that Jane Grant, under whatever her present alias, is right here in the Delmonico, Suite Fourteen Hundred. That shapes up—you. The tip says she came in yesterday from West Germany. That also shapes up—you. The tip says she's got hot rocks in her baggage. Maybe that shapes up you; maybe it doesn't. We're going to take a look. If you're Juliette Gaza legit, you won't mind our looking; if you're Juliette Gaza who's really Jane Grant, you'll holler holy hell which won't do you any good, not at all. Now how do you want us to look—which we're going to do anyway? With Juliette Gaza's permission? Or while one of my boys holds on to Jane Grant—while I do the looking?"

She did not want anyone looking. There were things in her trunks—and even the empty trunk—that she wanted no one, especially not a municipal policeman no matter how high his rank, to see. She considered declaring herself, stating exactly who she was and exhibiting her credentials, but what good would that do? If he believed her to be Jane Grant, then he would believe her credentials to be Jane Grant's forgeries and he would still insist upon a physical examination of her property.

"Mr. Parker, I must insist on my rights."

"You have no rights, Miss Grant."

"Gaza."

"Pick whatever name you like. You, lady, at this moment, at this time, at this point—*you* have no rights; the rights are ours."

The phone rang.

"May I?" she asked him.

"Please. Of course."

It was Gideon Rabin, enthusiastic. Not the protocol-Rabin, enmeshed in amenities, but a Rabin like a boy full of a secret that he can finally impart to a friend. It was not Rabin the diplomat, but a fervent Rabin fairly gushing. "Miss Gaza? I'm delighted you're there. Miss Gaza, I have happy news. Anna Stryker. So much better this morning, unbelievable. As the doctor said, it can happen. Concussion. Seems so perfectly recovered. He was there early this morning, just amazed, Dr. Vernon. And was back this forenoon, and just left my office here at the consulate. He says you can see her tomorrow, talk to her tomorrow, hates to keep them in bed when not necessary. Doesn't believe in invalidism, Dr. Vernon. Isn't that beautiful, Miss Gaza, just wonderful? Miss Gaza? Are you there, Miss Gaza? Hello? Hello!"

"Please, a moment," she said. She put her hand over the mouthpiece, looked toward the detective. "Mr. Parker, have you ever heard of Gideon Rabin? Of the Israeli consulate?"

"Hell yes. Of course. I know him well. Who doesn't in this town?"

A voice on the phone, somebody could trick it, a mimic. The man had refused the authenticity of her passport; he was a policeman and she knew policemen and understood. In his suspicion of her as Jane Grant, he had refused to accept her as Juliette Gaza; certainly he would not accept a disembodied voice, however familiar, as authentic. It would not do to have police suspicious of her, watching her from afar because their suspicions were somewhat allayed. Their suspicions would have to be totally allayed. She removed her hand from the mouthpiece.

"Mr. Rabin."

"Miss Gaza. I mean. I thought—"

"Mr. Rabin, could you come here, please? Now. Right away. It's quite important."

"But, Miss Gaza—"

"It's *most* important, sir. I promise not to hold you. Just a few minutes. A strange occurrence, inexplicable. I wouldn't impose on your time if it weren't—"

"Yes, of course, Miss Gaza. Yes."

"Please quickly, Mr. Rabin."

"Yes."

"Thank you." She hung up. She said, "Please be seated, gentlemen. Gideon Rabin—the man you know, as who doesn't as you said, in this town—will be here shortly. Perhaps he'll be able to convince you of your mistake, Mr. Parker."

The thick dark man flushed, smiled, made a bow, ungainly. Americans do not bow, they are not accustomed, they bow badly.

But the flush was even worse than the bow. He made a sound in his throat to cover it, drew a handkerchief, mopped his face.

"Please do sit down, Lieutenant Parker."

"Thank you, ma'am," he said.

℞ Twenty-two

THERE had been a crossfire of temperament in the kitchens of Café Ulrich and as peacemaker Tillie had been detained. She had called McGregor, informed him of her kitchen troubles. She had asked his indulgence, she would be a bit late for their appointment, and he had been affably sympathetic.

"No hurry, my dear. Any time before two."

"I'll be there long before two," she said. "I hope."

Now at twenty to one she rang his bell and he greeted her in sports shirt and slacks.

"Hello," she said. "Let's go rob a bank."

"Not yet. I'm working."

Work was in the library. A large table held many scattered papers and on the floor was a huge suitcase, open.

"What are we up to, Maestro?"

"We're in the process of robbing the bank."

The doorbell rang.

"Accomplices?" she asked.

"Yes, in a manner of speaking. But I expected it would be a phone call. Make yourself comfortable. I'll take him into the study."

"May I look at your, er, work?"

"Please do."

He opened the door for a blackly scowling Parker.

"Son of a bitch," Parker said.

"Good afternoon, Lieutenant. This way, please."

He led him to the study and closed the door. Parker's eyes were stormy.

"Louie," McGregor said, "if by some happenstance you got bilked in our horse trade, I assure you it wasn't meant."

"Bilked. Brother, it's just pure damn luck I'm not up against departmental charges. Pure damn luck I don't have the Commissioner himself chewing me out. Thank you very much, Inspector."

"What happened?"

"I got stomped, that's what happened. Gently. But stomped. Louie Parker charging in with the big mouth. Threatening illegal search and seizure. On advice from the eminent Inspector McGregor yet. Brother!"

"The lady balked?"

"Bilked. Balked. Always with the neat little words, the inspector. Brother, I got killed."

"That gentle lady?"

"She had gentle help. Only Gideon Rabin. I take it you know Gideon Rabin." The last was pure sarcasm.

"Rabin!"

"Brother, did I want to throw your name into the hopper. Just for the spite of it. Just to bail myself out. He knows his law, that Rabin. I'll say this. In his own way he was kind. He could have murdered me. He didn't. But he kept zinging it into me in his own gentle manner and he had me hemming and hawing like a goddamn jackass about international jewel thieves. . . ."

"My name didn't come into it, I trust."

"You trust right. But it would have served you right."

"Louie, please sit down. Let's start from scratch."

"I'll damn stand, if you don't mind."

"I don't understand about—Rabin. What's he got to do with any of this?"

"Look, let me make this short and sweet, and like that I can go back to my simple work of catching up with murderers. I got to your Juliette Gaza and gave her your song and dance about Jane Grant. She showed me her passport, told me she only came in yesterday from Germany—but to me she was Jane Grant and I made all the threats you suggested. Good thing I didn't go too far

118

or by God I'd sure have had my head handed to me. I was saved by the bell, the telephone bell. The phone rang, she talked, then told me that Gideon Rabin was coming over. That shut me up pretty good. I sat there with egg on my face and waited."

McGregor squinted. "You *are* talking about Gideon Rabin of the Israeli consulate."

"Damn right I am."

"I don't get it."

"You're about to get it right now, Inspector." There was a new expression in his dark eyes, a glint of glee. "Brother, wait'll you hear whom you're fooling around with." And now, palpably enjoying McGregor's reaction to tenterhooks, he paused, elaborately took out a cigar, elaborately lit it, blew on the match, and elaborately deposited it in an ashtray. "Well, sir, Rabin arrives, the lady gives him the me-Jane-Grant-him-Tarzan gist, and in his own gentle way—he knows his law, that baby—he cuts me up pretty good right in front of the two young cops I brought along with me. But then he kind of makes up for it. We know each other a long time, me and Rabin. Hell, I think it was you who introduced me to him. Like ages ago."

"I did."

"Now that gentle man turns it around with a compliment. I mean, a tacit compliment—confidence. He takes me into the bedroom and quietly straightens me out. Your Juliette Gaza is an Israeli operative. Shinbet, no less." Parker puffed his cigar, gleeful eyes observing the stunned McGregor. "You wanted information and you wanted verification. Okay, boss, you got them both."

It made sense. A lot of it made sense now.

"Thank you," McGregor finally murmured.

Parker nodded, smiled, made peace. All the glee was gone. "You look a little shook, Inspector."

"I'm shook, Lieutenant."

"How's the horse trading?"

"You couldn't have done better."

"No, I mean your part of it."

"Have you ever known me to break a promise, Louie?"

"No sir, I have not."

"I'll complete my part of our horse trade, I promise you, as quickly as I can manage."

"Good enough." They shook hands. "Sorry I shot my mouth off like I did." He grinned. "But I was burning when I came here." And laughed. "I cool easy, though."

McGregor took him to the door, they shook hands again, and Parker was gone. McGregor tapped himself for his cigarettes, found the pack, shook out a cigarette, snapped a light to it, and stood leaning against the door. It made sense; now he even knew who had recommended him—Gideon Rabin, naturally. A Shinbet agent on a job here in America. Part of the job—she was looking for Mannheim. Who better to accomplish that part of the job than a local operator? She had consulted with the man at the consulate and he had recommended ex-Inspector McGregor, now a private cop. It explained it all, her concocted cover-story and his nagging doubts about her because of that story, and on the Lubeck situation it put this Mannheim right in the middle and up to his neck. McGregor exhaled smoke in a long blue sigh, and went back to the study.

"What's all this with a signature?" Tillie asked. "Is your caller gone?"

"Yes."

"Are we going to rob a bank by forging a signature?"

"Many ways to skin a cat, and many different kinds of cats."

"Don't go esoteric on me, love. I mean if I'm to be your partner in crime. . . ." She waved toward the table. The many sheets had one writing, repeated over and over: the signature of Konrad Mannheim.

"I've put in hours on it," McGregor said.

"That's quite evident."

"Here look at this." He unfolded a paper, gave it to her. "A letter to Lubeck from Mannheim. Found it in there." He pointed. "Lubeck's suitcase." Now he took up a pen, scrawled the signature: *Konrad Mannheim.* "Compare," he said. "This signature and Mannheim's on the letter."

She looked, whistled. "Beautiful."

"Thank you. If you have the facility and you concentrate, it isn't too difficult. If they were blown up, if instruments were applied, if experts examined microscopically, I daresay they'd discover differences. But a cursory examination, it'll pass; and that's what it'll get—a cursory examination."

"Where?"

"The bank."

"What bank?"

"The bank which in a manner of speaking we're going to rob."

"Well, thank goodness for 'in a manner of speaking.' "

"Sit down, Tillie." She sat, and he sat. He lit another cigarette from the stub of the used one. "I want to tell you just what we're going to do."

She laughed. "Reminds me. A quote. Rather a classic. May I?"

"Sure."

"When they asked Willie Sutton why he robbed banks, his reply was spare but four-square: 'Because that's where the money is.' " She laughed again but McGregor remained dour. "Not funny?" she said. "Not apt?"

"Not now," he said.

"All yours, Maestro. I'm finished with classic remarks for the nonce."

He stood up, walked, talked with his head down.

"A little lecture on bank vaults. Once, long ago, I delivered a similar lecture to a group of bank presidents. You have a vault, Tillie; you know the procedure. It's like going to a savings bank for a withdrawal, but instead of your passbook you present your key. For the rest it's a quick comparison of signatures, period.

"When I lectured the bank presidents—I was on the force then—I requested a change in procedure. When it's a savings account, it's different: frequently there are many people, lines of people, and the teller simply doesn't have time for involved proceedings. But vaults are different: less people, more time. I suggested that instead of a mere signature comparison, there be a fingerprint system; that the man in charge be a fingerprint expert; that the owners of vaults have their fingerprints on file, and when they go to the vault their fingerprints are taken for comparison rather than signatures. My suggestion did not sit well with the presidents. It would be bad for the vault business. People do not like to submit to being fingerprinted, somehow it smacks of criminality.

"Vaults, by advertising and word of mouth, have been built up to be impregnable, and physically they are, but a vault is the easiest nut in the world to crack. All you need is the nerve, the key, the signature. Of course, you're locked in. If something goes wrong, you can't get out. That's what discourages the Willie Suttons from vault capers. No egress in case of emergency, and a good crook always maps out his line of retreat, the getaway route."

He slid into his chair, killed his cigarette.

"How often do you go to your vault, Tillie?"

"Not often. Who does?"

"Do you know the man there? Does he know you?"

"Of course not."

"At the risk of a pun, we're banking on that." His smile was wan. "Ready?" He looked at his watch, got up and got his jacket.

"You're banking that he doesn't know *me?*"

"That he doesn't know Mannheim; that it goes by rote, that the guards don't know the customers—how could they? A bank vault customer only comes once in a great while." He dropped the vault key into a pocket. "Ready?"

"I'm ready but just what's my purpose, Maestro?"

"Your purpose is three-fold, love." He lit a cigarette, smiled through the smoke. "First, your very proximity inspires my courage. Second, just in case something goes awry down there, you're witness to my intent which is to look, not to steal. I solemnly declare that intention here and now; we go to look, not to steal. And now in all good conscience you can swear I told you that— in the event of necessity. And third, your radiant presence will keep the guard's eyes off me and on you. They hardly look at the customers but in case anybody does he'll be looking at you rather than me. That'll ease it for Mannheim when he shows up. Can't say I'm not trying."

"You're trying."

"But whatever the circumstances when he shows—*he* can properly identify himself."

"Perhaps he's already shown."

"I doubt it. From what we've learned of him, he's a wise one, efficient. He had a damn busy day yesterday. Doesn't figure for precipitate action quite so soon after. Figures to give it a few days to cool off. I could be wrong. I hope not. Let's go give it a whirl."

☙ Twenty-three

THEY arrived at the Lincoln National Bank at five minutes after two. It was a part of the ground floor of a tall office building near the northeast corner of Madison Avenue at 44th Street. McGregor liked it. It was old-fashioned, unpretentious, dim and cavernous, the vaults to the left in the rear. There a robust, red-faced, armed young guard stood behind a steel-barred floor-to-ceiling gate. Smilingly McGregor waved the vault key and murmured, "May we?" Without comment the guard unlocked the gate, permitted them to enter, and locked the gate behind them. Before them was a steep flight of marble stairs. He took Tillie's hand. It was icy cold. They descended to a corridor at the end of which was another steel-barred floor-to-ceiling gate with a bell in the wall at its right. They could see through the bars into a room where another guard sat at a desk, and he saw them. There was no need to ring the bell. The guard rose slowly from his desk. He did not groan but McGregor could feel his inward groan. Arthritis, McGregor thought. The guard was an old one, a signature expert. These were the guards down there, McGregor knew: old-timers, experienced, uninterested, bored. He came toward them slowly, a pale, little, bow-legged man. McGregor waved the key but the guard hardly looked. He unlocked the gate, let them through, locked the gate, took them to the desk, motioned them to sit.

"Name?" he said.

"Mannheim. Konrad Mannheim."

The guard looked through an index file on his desk, brought out a card. Then he opened a book, said, "Sign here."

McGregor signed *Konrad Mannheim*.

The guard placed the card, which contained a signature, beneath the Konrad Mannheim signature McGregor had written, compared the signatures, grunted, returned the card to his desk file, closed the book, swung his swivel chair, consulted cards in a steel file, picked up a bunch of keys, said, "This way."

They followed him through narrow corridors of dull-shining steel, and then he stopped and they stopped with him. He inserted one of his keys into a lock, opened a big square door (a big one, McGregor thought, at least a foot square), said, "Now your key, only your key opens the inside door." McGregor gave him the key, he opened the inner lock, returned the key, said, "Want a room?"

"Yes."

McGregor pulled out the safety deposit box, long, rectangular, heavy, and they followed the little man to another area where he opened the door of a small room. "Here y' are," he said. "When you want me, just ring the bell."

The usual cubicle. Four chairs, a table, a door with a snap-lock. As McGregor, grunting, heaved the box to the table, Tillie snapped the lock of the door. He rolled his shoulder muscles to relax them: the damn box had been heavy; then he lifted the metal lid and heard Tillie's gasp and felt her breath at the side of his neck. Money! The box was stacked with neat packages of money, each package bound within a two-inch-wide bank-type brown paper strip. There were twenty such packages and each package contained fifty one-thousand-dollar bills. There was nothing else in the box.

"You're looking at a million dollars," he whispered.

"God, do I know it!"

"Tempted?"

"No."

"Afraid?"

"That's exactly correct."

"A fear to be applauded, love. Perfectly human. It's what keeps most of the world honest. Cynical, but cops learn that early in cop-life."

He packed the money back into the metal box, closed the lid, opened the door-lock, rang the bell. The little man came and the process was reversed. Then he opened the downstairs gate for them and they climbed the marble stairs and the red-faced guard opened the other gate and they walked through the bank into the sunshine of the busy normal workaday street and Tillie said, "Whew! Come back with me to the Ulrich and I'll buy you a drink. A series of drinks."

He looked at his watch. "No."

"What's the matter?"

"The job I'm being paid for."

"Pardon?"

"A change of plans."

"All of a sudden?"

"All of a sudden I'm nervous."

"The sight of all that money?"

"Somehow you don't believe it till you see it." His eyes were looking past her, toward the entrance of the bank. "Look, you go right ahead."

"You'll come by?"

"For dinner. We'll have dinner."

"See you later."

She went off in a cab, and he remained in the vicinity until the bank closed.

Tant il est vrai qu'il
faut changer de stratageme.

How true it is that it is
necessary to change the stratagem.

🎜 Twenty-four

DAVE called to say he would be a half hour early. "I'll buy you lunch."

"Lunch." She groaned. "We had a rather late breakfast, or don't you remember?"

He laughed. "I remember, I remember. But I'm hungry."

"All right. Fine. Lunch."

"I'll take you somewhere special."

"No. Downstairs here."

"You owe allegiance to the Delmonico?"

"I want to stay close. Rabin may call."

"Oh?"

"I've things to tell you. Anna Stryker. And more."

"More? Give me a hint."

"I had a visit from a policeman."

"The hell you did. What for?"

"Tell you when I see you."

"Two-thirty?"

"Fine. I'll meet you in the lobby."

She went down at 2:25, to the desk.

"Juliette Gaza," she said. "Suite Fourteen Hundred. If anyone calls me, I'll be in the dining room."

"Yes, Madame."

Jordon arrived promptly at 2:30, handsome, well-dressed, and in the dining room they had drinks and he ate while she nibbled. Ate like a horse, a strong, healthy man, while she filled him in on current events.

". . . so much for the lieutenant, a mistake, an annoyance, a misadventure. What's important to us—Anna Stryker. I've an appointment with her at Rabin's apartment for tomorrow noon, unless the doctor calls it off."

"Any chance he will?"

"Rabin doesn't think so. But that's why I'm staying close. Any change, he'll call me."

And just then her name was sounded through the public address system. "Juliette Gaza. Miss Juliette Gaza."

"Oh no," she breathed.

"Fingers crossed," he said.

She raised a hand aloft. The captain saw her. The metallic voice ceased.

She glanced at her watch. It was five minutes after three.

The captain came, carrying a jack-telephone.

"A moment, Madame."

He plugged it into a wall outlet, carefully arranged the long wire, placed the phone on the table.

"Voilà," he said, bowed, and went away.

She picked up the receiver. "Yes?"

"Miss Gaza?"

"Juliette Gaza."

"McGregor."

"Ah. So?"

"May I see you?"

"Of course. When?"

"I'd like as soon as possible."

"Very well. When?"

"Fifteen minutes?"

"Excellent. My suite?"

"If you wish."

"My suite. Fifteen minutes."

"See you then." He hung up.

She replaced the receiver.

"Rabin?" Jordan said.

"No. Rabin's detective."

Suite 1400. Conversation sparse. They waited impatiently. He smoked his pipe. She sipped brandy. Kept looking at her watch.

"Fifteen minutes he said. So where the hell is he?"

"Rough this time of day, Julie. The taxis, it's their change-up time. And the traffic in New York, it's always murder. This the first you've heard from him?"

"The first."

"You didn't call him to inquire?"

"Oh the *hell*, Dave. When? He only just got it, my God. You're in the business. You've got to give a man time—to move, roam, look, inquire. Christ!"

"Yeah."

He sat, smoked.

She roved the room, her fingernails in her palms, stopped occasionally for a fleeting glance out the window, stopped for a sip of brandy from the glass on the table, was beginning to feel the brandy, was beginning goddamnit to get a heartburn, and then froze at the ring of the bell. And recovered. And went quickly to the door.

"Mr. McGregor."

"Miss Gaza."

And, damn, was so pleased at the sight of him. Tall. Powerful. White-haired but young-eyed. The smooth ruddy complexion, the bones of the face, the black eyebrows, the cut of the jaw, the damn imperious look of an eagle.

"Please come in."

"Thank you."

And the walk of him. Like the legs had nothing to do with the body. Lithe. Like on springs. Like the walk of an animal, a huge cat, panther, lion; graceful without purpose, a natural rhythm.

"Mr. McGregor. Mr. Jordan. I believe I mentioned my fiancé."

"Yes, you did. Dave Jordan."

Dave stood up. They shook hands.

"Mr. McGregor," Dave said.

"My pleasure, Mr. Jordan."

"May I offer some brandy?" she said.

"Yes, if you please," the detective said.

"You'll have to forgive the glass."

"It's what's in the glass."

"For that I won't ask forgiveness."

She brought a glass, poured brandy, watched while he sipped.

"So?" she said.

"Excellent."

"Thank you."

The detective lit a cigarette, took his glass, sat.

Dave sat. She sat.

Silence, a rather awkward silence, but damn woman she enjoyed it. Two of them. Two terribly handsome men and she alone with them. Enjoying the silence she drank brandy, then broke it. She was not here for enjoyment. Her business here was business.

"You have a report for me, Mr. McGregor?"

His eyes moved to Dave Jordan, then back to her.

"Yes."

128

"If you please."

"Miss Gaza. . . ." He smiled. "I mean . . . confidential." He inhaled cigarette smoke, and again his eyes moved to Dave. "No offense, Mr. Jordan."

"If you please," she said. "I should have told you. Dave knows everything. All. He knows that I retained you and why I retained you. I have no secrets from him. Please feel free, entirely free, Mr. McGregor."

The detective drank brandy as though he needed it. She stood up, replenished his glass, sat.

"Whatever it is you have to tell, Mr. McGregor, you may tell it in Mr. Jordan's presence. If however it would be more comfortable for you to tell me alone, then of course Mr. Jordan will leave us." Jordan smiled, stood up. "Your choice, Mr. McGregor," she said. "However it's more comfortable for you. But whatever you do tell me, I shall in turn relay to Mr. Jordan. He can have it first hand from you or second hand from me. But whatever's more comfortable for you, Mr. McGregor."

"The lady's paying the freight," the detective said to Dave. "I'm her man for hire; she says you know and I'm quite as comfortable with you as without you. If she prefers you hear first hand. . . ."

"I do," she said.

"Then please sit down, Mr. Jordan."

"Thank you," Dave said and sat.

"Mr. McGregor," she said.

"Konrad Mannheim," the detective said. "Quite a man, this Mannheim, as I've learned from my brief but intensive investigation."

"Quite," she said.

"Miss Gaza, last evening the police found a murdered man who appeared to be the victim of a mugging. He was about forty, a big blond man. He wore his hair crew-cut, he had a Van Dyke beard and a scar over his right cheekbone. All his possessions had been taken. The police have no idea as to his name or identity."

She looked toward Dave and quickly back to the detective.

"He was found, Miss Gaza, under the stairs in the rear of 218 Central Park South."

"Mannheim!" she blurted.

"Pardon?"

"No, nothing," she stammered. "Please excuse the interruption, Mr. McGregor."

He tamped out his cigarette, sipped brandy. "Miss Gaza, is it your idea that Mannheim committed this murder?"

She hesitated. Then: "Yes—if the man is who I think he is."

"The man's name—Ludwig Lubeck."

"Just a moment, please." Jordan took his pipe out of his mouth. "If the police don't know the man's name, how do you know it, Mr. McGregor?"

The detective disregarded him. "Lubeck," he said to her. "Is that the man you thought?"

"Are you sure—Lubeck?" The detective nodded. "Then there's no question in my mind," she said. "And found on the very premises. Mannheim killed him. I can't prove it of course, but I'd swear."

"You'd swear wrong, Miss Gaza. I killed him."

Her mouth opened but she did not speak. She shifted her glance to Dave. His eyes were fastened like claws on McGregor's face.

"I haven't told the police yet," McGregor said. His tone was quite mild. "I shall in time, at the proper time." He lit a cigarette and now he looked directly at Dave. "I trust neither of you will breach this confidence. The killing was an act of self-defense and done in the course of my investigation on behalf of Miss Gaza."

"You can depend on me, Mr. McGregor," Dave said.

And now for the first time a hint of acerbity. "I have no wish to depend on you, Mr. Jordan. On the contrary it is you—if you are party to Miss Gaza's interests—who must depend on me. The object of my employ is to ascertain the whereabouts of Konrad Mannheim. I'm under the impression that such employ was meant to be private and confidential, otherwise Miss Gaza would have gone to the police."

"Yes, true," she said.

"If now I went to the police with my story, or they learned it from other sources, I would have to divulge all the facts, and newspapermen are most alert when it comes to sensational facts. Konrad Mannheim would be put upon public notice that he is being sought. I doubt whether Miss Gaza would approve of that."

"I wouldn't," she said.

He was still looking at Dave. "I take it you're working with Miss Gaza on this enterprise?"

"Yes he is. Very closely." And caught her lower lip in her teeth and instantly released it. A bright man, brilliant. While casually imparting information, he was eliciting information. She had made a total admission to an experienced detective. So all right, what harm? He had probably divined by now—possibly even had facts to sustain him—that his job was not the simple matter of finding an ex-husband delinquent in his alimony. At this stage to insult his intelligence would in effect be insulting her own. "Yes, Mr. McGregor." She smiled. "Mr. Jordan is a full partner in what you call my enterprise. I assure you we understand that a breach of your confidence would be detrimental to our interests."

"Thank you." He tapped ash from his cigarette. "My encounter with this Lubeck happened in Mr. Mannheim's apartment. From the physical evidence in that apartment Mannheim has no intention to return there, at least not permanently. All his clothes are out, everything. On the other hand, I do believe your Mr. Mannheim is still among us."

"Why, Mr. McGregor?" She tried to keep her voice in control.

"I left Lubeck, quite dead, in the apartment. He was found hours later, quite dead, out of the apartment. A corpse doesn't transport himself. But I have a better reason. A million better reasons."

"That's a lot of reasons," Dave Jordan said.

"Lubeck and Mannheim were joined in a crime of rather large proportions. Rather. A million bucks worth. That's large. Embezzled over a long period by Lubeck in Buenos Aires from the notorious National Socialist League of Argentina. The names they give themselves. Socialist. There's about as much socialism in the League as there's atheism in the Vatican. Anyway, that million bucks is right here in the United States."

Dave Jordan slammed to his feet.

"How the hell do you know this!"

"Sit down!"

Silence. Tableau. Please God, she prayed. The one standing.

The one sitting. Blue eyes looking up. Black eyes blazing down. Locked. Two of them, strong, powerful personalities. Please God no, she prayed. Outburst now, clash, would be fatal. A wrong word by either of them, a wrong gesture, and all her work, her purpose, could be demolished. If the detective walked out on them, their work was ended. He had a murder on his conscience. Self-defense he said, but a killing. If he got up and went out and informed the police—ended.

Dave! Please! She was silent.

He moved. Backed down. Sat.

Thank you, Dave. Thank you, God.

He put his pipe in his mouth. She heard his teeth grinding on the stem. And the other one waited. And Dave took the pipe from his mouth. And laid it on the table. Male animals. They had a language of their own.

Thank you, Dave. Wise. Male animals. A gesture.

"Mr. Jordan, my purpose here is to report the results of my investigations to Miss Gaza. Not the methods of my investigations. Is that clear?"

"Yes." Like a belch. A gut word. Croaking sounds, up from the viscera. Damn male animals. "Yes, Mr. McGregor. Perfectly clear."

Now the cold blue eyes were on her. "As I was saying, Miss Gaza, that money, a formidable sum, is right here in the United States. It's in a safe deposit box in the Lincoln National Bank on Madison Avenue and Forty-fourth Street. The box is in Konrad Mannheim's name and I know the money is still there. He won't let it rot there, will he? It's all his now, with Lubeck dead. I have information that your Mr. Mannheim intends to leave the country, but I don't think he'll leave a million dollars behind him, do you? As Mr. Shakespeare said in *Much Ado About Nothing:* 'Bait the hook well; this fish will bite.' Well, this fish has baited his own hook. He'll rise to the bait, and in short order in my opinion. From here on out, quite simple. Station me if you please, or yourself, or Mr. Jordan, or whomever else you think properly capable, outside the Lincoln National Bank and you'll catch up with your Mr. Mannheim. How do you want it, Miss Gaza?"

"Dave," she said. "Mr. Jordan. Dave'll do it."

"Yes," Dave said. "And I'm properly capable, believe me, Mr. McGregor."

"I believe you," McGregor said. "Nine to three outside the Lincoln National Bank and you're bound to catch up with him." He pressed out his cigarette, smiled, stood up. "That's about it except for another little matter, somewhat tangential, but it may be of interest to you, Miss Gaza."

"Whatever you say is of interest to me, Mr. McGregor." She said it feminine, coyly, flirtatiously, despite Dave and to hell with Dave. Dave was a co-worker, not a lover. Dave, as co-worker, was also a pleasant, momentary affair and Dave well knew that and if he didn't, the hell with Dave. She had a lurking desire for this tall, blue-eyed, cold-eyed, imperious man, and she knew it showed and made no effort to conceal it.

"Mannheim had a sweetheart, a paramour," McGregor said. "Gertrude Stryker in a neat little pad in an apartment house at Fifty-eight Beverly Road, Flushing, Queens. I went there in your interests, Miss Gaza, to inquire about Mannheim. I didn't get any answers."

"Gertrude Stryker?" she said, thoughts of love, personal pleasure, secret moments with this strange man all obliterated, all pre-empted by profession, business. "Why no answers, Mr. McGregor?"

"I found her in her refrigerator," he said, and quickly told of his experience in apartment 3D, 58 Beverly Road, Flushing, Queens. "I know nothing about her except, quick check of the apartment, there's a sister, Anna Stryker, supposed to be coming from Australia to the U.S. en route to Israel. Figures our friend Mannheim done her in, cleaning up loose ends. A small hole in the head, my estimate a .22, not a professional's weapon. There were some bank books around, savings bank books. If you're interested in details, Miss Gaza, check it out with the Queens police. I called it in, anonymous. And you, Mr. Jordan. If and when you catch up with him, he may be carrying a .22. General rule, amateur murderers aren't disposed to get rid of weapons; it's usually a weapon they're accustomed to, fond of; and once they plan out a murder and it goes off without a hitch, somehow they can't conceive of any possible future involvement. He figures to be armed with his .22, so be careful. If he is, and you can get it away from him, we'd all appreciate. Ballistics. It could be proof positive." He moved toward the door. "That's about it, Miss Gaza. Full report up to date."

"The balance of your fee?"

"We haven't caught up with him yet, have we?" He opened the door. "Until then I'm at your service. Feel free to call."

The door closed and he was gone.

"Quite a man," she said.

Dave said, "A typical son of a bitch cop."

℞ Twenty-five

HE took a cab to Homicide. Lieutenant Parker was out. "Gone for the day?" he asked.

"No sir, Inspector," the sergeant said. "Out on a job. He'll be back."

"I'll wait."

"Wait in his room if you like, Inspector."

"Thank you."

Old policemen never fade away, they die. Like the United States Senate, it was a special kind of club. Once a cop you're regarded by cops as a cop, always. And your rank stays with you, and the respect for rank. Ex-Inspector McGregor, here Inspector McGregor, waited alone in Detective-Lieutenant Parker's office. He was tired. He sat in a hard chair, chin down, dozing. It was an hour before Parker arrived.

"Hi, Inspector."

"Hi," McGregor said. "You look like I feel."

Dark bristles of beard were beginning to sprout on the lieutenant's cheeks, his jowls hung loose, there were circles under his eyes.

"They keep murdering each other." He grinned, wiped his face with a handkerchief, sank heavily in the swivel chair behind his desk. "You come to complete your half of our bargain?"

"Not quite. I've come for assistance in the completion of my half of the bargain."

"Here we go."

"Stakeout."

"Stakeout, hey? Nice. Music to these old ears. Sounds like you're moving in close, hey, Inspector?"

McGregor lit a cigarette. "I'll need a lot of men, but only two at a time for a couple of hours. Like that I won't be tying up too many of your people. They do their trick of duty with me and then they're back for duty with you. And I'll need a lot of cars, always change-ups, half of them taxis, I figure, half private cars."

"Go slow, Inspector."

"Nine to three, in the environs of the Lincoln National Bank on Madison by Forty-fourth. There'll always be two cars, parked or double-parked, one a cab, one a private car. I'll always be the passenger in one of them. The passenger in the rear doesn't show, but the car does and the driver does; that's why the change-up in cars and drivers."

"Keep going, but stay slow, Inspector."

"I'll be watching, but there'll be another guy watching and I don't want him to know. Say I'm in the cab. When I get the opportunity, I slip out of the cab and into the private car, parked or double-parked nearby. Motors always running, driver always in place, so no trouble with cops about traffic problems. If trouble, then our driver identifies himself as a cop working and that's the end of the trouble."

"Good enough so far. Keep it slow."

"There'll have to be an identification mark on our cars and cabs, so I'll know. A half-inch square of flesh-colored adhesive tape on the lower left-hand corner of the windshield. No one in the world figures to notice that except me looking. The cabs will always have to have the flag down, occupied, you know? If somebody wants him for a hail, his passenger went into one of the office buildings and he's waiting."

"Right."

"Okay, I'm out of the cab and in the private car. Now the cab takes off, comes back to home base, and a different cab with a different driver comes back to me. When I get the opportunity, I shift out of the private car to the new cab, the private car comes back to home base, and I get a new private car and new driver."

"I dig," Parker said. "You're in operation. When does it start?"

"I'll be here tomorrow morning at eight. I want to be at the bank by nine."

"How long does this go?"

"A week I figure, maybe more, maybe less."

"Good enough. You're in business."

"Business for both of us."

"If you say so, Inspector."

"See you in the morning."

"Good luck."

"Thank you."

"To both of us."

Home. Weary. He put up water to boil, slid bread into the toaster. He made three-minute eggs, broke them into a tall glass, dropped in a dab of butter, shook in salt, beat with a long spoon till foamy. He cut the toast into small squares, added them to the egg mixture. He ate standing up, the glass near his mouth, feeding like an invalid on a soft diet, spooning in the soaked squares of toast. Finished, he put the glass in the sink under the faucet, let it wash in cold water, then hot, then turned off the tap.

He undressed, weighed himself, scowled at the scale.

In the bedroom he turned the phone-wheel to loud, set the clock alarm for eight, said good night to nobody, pulled up the cover and was immediately asleep.

No ring of the phone. Awoke to the alarm. Turned it off. Said good morning in the evening to nobody. Got out of bed, refreshed. Showered, shaved, stood on the scale and did not scowl. Why is it we weigh less after a sleep? He dressed, had a sip of sherry, and went to Café Ulrich, arriving there at nine o'clock, their usual dinner hour, after the customer rush. She had guests. A painter from New Mexico who once upon a time had had an imbroglio with a President about a commissioned portrait that displeased the client, and the painter's charming wife, and an ebullient conductor of a symphony orchestra, and the ebullient conductor's charming wife. The dinner was excellent, the company excellent, the conversation excellent. And then the guests were gone and he stayed until closing and then upstairs he set an alarm again, for seven o'clock, but awoke before the alarm rang and moved carefully not to wake her and dressed and then bent to her, to soft warmth and quiet breathing, and kissed her forehead, not waking her, and went out into the new day and to Homicide.

℞ Twenty-six

JULIETTE GAZA dressed in shades of brown today—a tan lightweight suit and tan sculptured stockings, a dark-brown blouse, dark-brown pumps, and a large dark-brown leather bag —arrived at five minutes after twelve at the penthouse apartment on East 70th Street. Aliza Rabin opened the door to her ring.

"Miss Gaza, so pleasant of you to come. How are you?"

"You, Mrs. Rabin?"

"Fine, fine, come in, do come in." And in the living room asked, "A spot of lunch, Miss Gaza?"

"No, thank you."

"A drink, perhaps? Coffee?"

"Nothing, thank you. You're very kind. Dr. Vernon, he's here?"

"Oh yes, of course, with Gideon in his study. This way, dear."

"Miss Stryker, how is she?"

"Wonderful, just wonderful, perfectly normal, what a change. Leo had assured us it wasn't *really* serious—Leo, Dr. Vernon. But we, us—what shall I say?—we're only, laymen. I mean not doctors. How she looked just a few days ago, so dreadful. He told

137

us, I mean to expect the change, but doctors, you know. . . ."

"She's in bed?"

"Bed! Oh no." And laughed. "Out on the terrace, taking the sun. And yesterday too. And eats! So beautiful. A little woman, but a marvelous appetite." And Aliza Rabin stopped suddenly, took her wrist, and she saw the shine of tears in the woman's eyes. "We're so gratified, it's so gratifying." And smiled, the rainbow smile of suppressed tears. "This way, dear. Come along, Miss Gaza."

In the study, the men stood up.

"Miss Gaza," Dr. Vernon said.

"Doctor." She smiled, nodded.

"Miss Gaza, so good," Rabin said. "Aliza, dear, do make Leo another drink. A stinger-man, Miss Gaza, how do you like that? Stingers in the afternoon, our doctor. And do amuse him for a few minutes while I take Miss Gaza away. Tell him one of your risky jokes; I mean that risky in the French sense, Leo. She's very good at dirty jokes, my Aliza. Please, Miss Gaza." He touched her elbow, opened a door, took her through to a little office.

"What about Stryker, the other Stryker?" she asked.

"All in order." There was no lilt in his voice now. "I made the inquiries in behalf of our Stryker, she's the only next of kin. My lawyer, man by the name Hugh Massey—he'll be in touch with you—he's filed as attorney representing her. Police want to talk with her, but we've stalled them off, claiming she's too ill. What with you coming, we just can't pile her with one thing on top of the other, can we? Massey knows about you, of course, and he'll keep you apprized all the way."

"She's been told?"

"Told?" He blinked. "What?"

The poor guy, mixed in the middle, so obviously stalling, she was sorry for him. "About Gertrude," she said.

He closed his eyes, shook his head, opened his eyes.

"I just didn't, damnit, have the heart."

"My job, eh?"

"I don't envy the job. Any of your jobs, Miss Gaza." A crooked little smile. "Each to his own."

"The doctor knows why I'm here?"

"Yes."

"I'm going to talk to her about quite terrible matters, Mr. Rabin, and I'm also going to break it to her about her sister. The doctor knows all this?"

"He knows you're from our government, that you must, your job, your work, subject her, possibly, to strenuous interrogation."

"He approves?"

"I informed him you wouldn't be here unless it were a matter of dire necessity."

"Dire," she said grimly. "An excellent choice of word. He approves?"

"In this area of choosing words—no, he doesn't approve. Consents." He smiled accommodatingly, unhappily. "Upon pressure from me, he consents."

"Yes," she nodded. "A distressing situation, any way you look at it. I don't like it, Mr. Rabin, but my personal likes or dislikes are of no consequence. The matter is urgent, the weight of years presses heavily, and I'm no more than a cog in the vast, complicated machinery of justice." She sighed. "Ready now, if you please." And smiled. "I've had to—pump myself up for this moment. Am I expressing it badly? Gear myself, rise to a pitch. But to tell the truth, I'm nervous as hell."

"It certainly doesn't show, Miss Gaza."

"Look, is it possible—I'd rather not, now, face your wife. Or Dr. Vernon. Is there some way . . . ?"

He pointed to a side door. "Yes, I can take you through there."

"Please, a moment." She opened her leather handbag, switched on a transistor-powered tape recorder, shut the bag. "Ready now," she said.

℞ Twenty-seven

HE led her through a long narrow corridor to a glass door in the rear. He opened the door, motioned for her to precede him, joined her on a huge flagstoned terrace surrounded by high brick walls like ramparts. The sun was warm, pleasant, and there was a soft little breeze. A perfect, pretty, peaceful June afternoon.

Quite in the center of the terrace on a flower-designed tufted-mattressed chaise longue Anna Stryker reclined in a sitting position, eyes closed as though asleep, her hands folded in her lap. She was stockingless in thonged leather sandals, blue slacks, and a blue blouse open at the neck. Black hair, swept up from little ears, was festooned in a blue ribbon. To her right was a patio table on which were tall glasses and a glass pitcher full almost to the brim with ice and an amber liquid. Far to her left, in a corner of the terrace, were many more little patio tables and chairs.

At the sound of the heels clacking on the flagstones, she opened her eyes, turned her head, smiled at the approaching Rabin. She had little teeth, very white. She had a little nose and a little mouth and a little face—she herself was so little—but her eyes, black, limpid, upslanted, were enormous. Is it a rule of life? thought Juliette Gaza. So many of the little people have tremendous eyes.

"How are you, dear?" Rabin said.

"I think I was asleep." She giggled, a full sound from the throat. A clear voice but a soft voice, slow, a little gasp in it. "That's so much I do lately, I'm embarrassed to say—sleep."

"Anna, this is Miss Gaza, Juliette Gaza. Miss Gaza, Miss Stryker, Anna Stryker."

"How do you do."

"How do you do."

His laugh had effort. "I warned you she'd be coming to visit."

"Warned?" Anna Stryker said. "He's so sweet." The black eyes were now fully on her. "They've been so good to me, so kind."

"She's come all the way from Europe, just to talk to you."

"Yes, you told me, Mr. Rabin."

"About what *you* told me, in the beginning, in my office."

The black eyes closed, opened. "Yes."

"Excuse me," he said. He went away, came back with a patio table which he placed close to the chaise longue at Anna's left, went away and came back again with a chair. "Please, Miss Gaza," he said, making a gesture at the chair.

"Thank you." She sat, put her handbag on the table.

He came around with the pitcher and a glass. "Refreshment, iced tea," he said and made a little bow. "And now perforce" —and smiled—"I withdraw and leave you two to your own tender mercies."

The glass door opened and closed and they were alone.

A good man, a wise man, a diplomat, the new consul general to be—she knew his last words were meant for her: tender mercies. She crossed her legs, smiled without meaning, as brown eyes and black eyes, vis-à-vis, did appraisal. Woman to woman, always difficult. Woman to man, or man to woman, always, somehow, easier. Juliette Gaza was an experienced campaigner. She continued to smile, without meaning. How different the woman looked now as contrasted to when she had last seen her there in bed. The patch of adhesive on the forehead was smaller and narrower now, the face had a glow from the sun; she was alive, turned in recovery, but the eyes, damn, I can swear—experienced campaigner—are antagonistic. Why? Hell, why? Go easy, Julie.

"Miss Stryker."

"Anna. Please, Anna. I am not one for formalities."

"Anna, you came to Mr. Rabin of your own volition."

"Yes."

"About Konrad Mannheim."

The eyes were hooded now, half-lidded, and the mouth tight as the woman nodded. There was a shine of perspiration in the hollows by the nose.

"Anna. About Konrad Mannheim?"

"No!"

A pause. Recollecting. "Yes, quite correct. You did not mention the name Konrad Mannheim to Mr. Rabin—you said Konrad Kassel. Yet, just a moment ago when I asked if you came to Mr. Rabin about Konrad Mannheim, you nodded. You nodded, Anna, didn't you?"

No answer. The huge black eyes were wide open now.

"Anna, are you aware that the man Konrad Mannheim here in America is the same man who was SS Colonel Konrad Kassel, commander of Camp Number Six in Auschwitz?"

No answer, but in the corners of the eyes by the bridge of the nose, the beginning of tears.

Juliette Gaza sat back, took a sip of the iced tea, found it too sweet, put down the glass. She was on course, she had asked the preliminary questions exactly as she had intended. She had asked quickly, bluntly, about Konrad Mannheim, not Konrad Kassel, with purpose, and had got the assent, however tentative, she had hoped for. After McGregor's visit, she had given long thought to the process of the interrogation upon which she was now here embarked. In all the many years in Australia the woman had not offered one word about Nazi war criminals—Kassel's dossier contained every single fact bearing on the case—yet within ten days of her arrival in America she had come to the consulate with the proffer of information regarding one Konrad Kassel. In America, Konrad Kassel was Konrad Mannheim and the detective had reported that Gertrude Stryker was Mannheim's paramour and Mannheim's paramour was Anna's sister. Sisters are not wont to confide in sisters about illicit relationships; had Anna seen Mannheim in her sister's company and recognized him as Kassel?—a simple recognition except for the few age-wrinkles in the face and the gray in the temples—and had she then impetuously come to the consulate offering her story? Had she then told Gertrude and been *told* by Gertrude? Was that then the meaning of her reluctance now: the sacrifice of her silence to the sister's happiness? That sacrifice would hold; she knew nothing of the sister's death. And it was more than just reluctance now. She had been here, in Rabin's apartment, since her accident, and was recovered, yet she had offered no part of the story she had come to the consulate to tell, else Rabin would have made report to Suite 1400 at the Delmonico.

142

She sipped again of the too-sweet iced tea.

The woman's face was to the sun, her eyes closed.

"Anna."

The eyes opened.

"Anna, I believe you know from Mr. Rabin who I am, why I'm here."

The eyes hooded again, the face nodding slowly.

"Have you had a change of heart?"

The lips coming together like a kiss, the jaw muscles knotted.

"You went to the consulate, to Mr. Rabin; you said you had a story of a war criminal, Konrad Kassel, and you were promised a proper agent to whom to tell that story. I'm that agent, Anna. Have you had a change of heart?"

The mouth, dryly, loosened; the tip of the tongue flicked to its corners. "I—prefer not—not to speak."

"Because of your sister?"

The face jolted back as though struck; the knees came up in a rigid position of fright, a recoil. She was so terribly sorry for the poor woman.

"Anna, she's dead. Gertrude." The woman's mouth opened round. "This falls to me, Anna. To inform you. My duty. I must. Gertrude Stryker was murdered. We believe Mannheim murdered her."

Curiously now, a relaxation. The knees came down. The face tilted sidewise. "Miss Gaza, you are from the government. You have your work. You came to finish what I began." A sigh. A wan smile. "For reasons of my own—yes, involving my sister—I no longer choose to speak, to bring back the past. You on your part, however—I understand. The duty you mention. You must use whatever trick you can. I understand." She closed her eyes. "I will not speak. I have nothing to say."

Juliette Gaza stood up.

"Excuse me."

She crossed the terrace, opened the glass door, walked the long corridor, opened the side door of the little office, went to the other door, flung it open. Eyes turned up to her.

Aliza Rabin, the doctor, and Gideon Rabin were seated having coffee. Rabin put down his cup. "Miss Gaza?"

"Please. Please in here, Mr. Rabin."

He went quickly with her into the office.

"You're going to have to tell her, Mr. Rabin."

"Tell . . . ?"

She looked about. "And perhaps—a stimulant?"

"Yes." His hand was trembling as it touched the knob of a cabinet. He brought out a bottle of brandy.

"She doesn't believe me," Juliette Gaza said. "About the sister. She thinks it—the death—what I told her—some kind of ruse. To overcome her objection."

"Objection to what?"

"She refuses to talk."

"But why?"

"Please, Mr. Rabin."

"Yes."

Anna Stryker had her knees up again, her arms encircling them, her hands tightly clasped. She watched as they approached, Rabin nervously smiling, nodding, holding the bottle by its neck like a club.

He went to one side of the chaise longue, Juliette Gaza to the other. As she sat again, he opened the bottle at the table on Anna's right, poured brandy into three glasses, hesitated over them, fished out a cigarette and lit it.

"Anna," Juliette Gaza said, "I meant our conversation to be private. And it shall be, I promise, once we get started. For now —please, Mr. Rabin. Please tell it as completely as possible, sir."

"Anna . . ." he began. He swallowed, his Adam's apple bobbing. He picked up a glass, drank brandy, put it down. "Gertrude Stryker," he said. "Apartment 3D, Fifty-eight Beverly Road, Borough of Queens, not in the telephone book, an unlisted phone number. A three room apartment, living room, bedroom, and kitchen. Gertrude Stryker was found dead in her apartment, a bullet through her forehead, assailant unknown, it is now a police matter. I didn't have the heart to tell you, Anna; you just recovering; you would learn it soon enough from Miss Gaza." He paused. The woman was looking up at him, silently. "There's reason to believe she was killed by Konrad Mannheim who is the man you mentioned to me as Konrad Kassel, but that is Miss Gaza's province to explain to you. I—and my lawyer—are taking care of your interests. We've already checked Sydney and know you are the one next of kin. Her assets, aside from clothes, furniture and such, are one hundred and sixty-two dollars in cash and three savings bank books showing a total of twenty-seven thousand eight hundred fifty dollars and twenty-three cents. There are also several letters from you to her about your coming to visit in the United States before you take up permanent residence in Israel. The police are holding all of that as temporary custodians. The police want to talk to you but I've held them off, pleading your illness, pending your talk with Miss Gaza."

The woman's poise was remarkable. Not a change in expression, not a flicker of emotion, no tears. True, she had had time to prepare herself during the short interim when she Juliette had gone out for Rabin; nevertheless, remarkable. She had not at all been that contained while they were skirmishing in the preliminaries, but there are persons like that, they can call on inner resources, they seem to grow stronger, firm up in the face of strong events. She will make a good witness, Juliette Gaza thought, if—*if.* . . .

Rabin stood over them helplessly. She caught his eye, he understood. "Ladies." He inclined his head in a little bow and went away and she heard the glass door close and kept her posture, held the mood, her eyes on the black eyes staring up at her steadfastly.

"Forgive me, Miss Gaza."

"Not at all."

"I am ready now."

"Thank you."

A little smile. "Don't you—want to make notes?"

"There are notes being made." She pointed to her handbag. "In there. A tape recorder."

"I see. First, please, to explain." She stretched out on the chaise longue, her eyes slanted now, the lids lowered against the shine of the sun. "I am here in the States for a time as you know, you heard, my letters to Gertrude, before going away to live the rest of my life with my own people in Israel. My passport, visas, all are in order; they are here in this house now, all; Mr. Rabin has brought all my things. They have been so good to me, so kind, Mr. and Mrs. Rabin. You know?"

"Yes."

"There is this evening I am visiting with Gertrude in her apartment in Queens on Long Island. A man comes, an unexpected visitor. Mannheim she introduces, Mr. Konrad Mannheim, a former employer where she worked, Mannheim Incorporated. I recognize him and remember: there is much I forgot, as I shall tell you. He is not Mannheim, he is Kassel, SS Colonel Konrad Kassel of Camp Number Six, and as if he is the key to a locked door, remembering him I remember all, but I say nothing, and then when he leaves I ask Gertrude to drive me home. I say nothing to her."

"Why?"

"Difficult to answer. Please understand—I shall explain—these are sudden terrifying recollections, forgotten in childhood, a sick childhood, and now all at once they are all around me, overwhelming. I must think. Alone. What reason to bring her in? It is for me, not for her. I must think."

"You say she drove you. She owns a car?"

"A rented car. And so after a sleepless night, the next day I go to the consulate. He is always so kind, courteous, Mr. Rabin. Tells me an agent from Shinbet will be in touch with me. A day. A few days. After so many years it is not an emergency, of course. There is no pressure. And the day after, it is Saturday, and Gertrude comes in the morning, we have an appointment for shopping. I am sick with recollection. I am drinking—I am not accustomed to drink. I tell her I have been to the consulate and I tell her why and I tell her that an agent from Shinbet will come to me for all my information. She tells me I am crazy—Mannheim! —I am crazy. A bitter word for me, Miss Gaza—crazy. I was, as I shall explain, for many years in Australia in a mental institution, a sanitorium. But I know I am not crazy, I *know* I am not—I have recognized this man! It is clear to me now how closely she questioned me: how much (which was little) did I tell Rabin at the consulate, and did I mention the name Mannheim? I did not. He was not Mannheim to me; he was Konrad Kassel. As for Mannheim, they would question *her* about Mannheim; I did not know a Mannheim; he was Konrad Kassel. We argued but arguments end, and then she was kind to me—perhaps too kind, soothing the crazy one—and we got ready to go out for our shopping. My apartment—perhaps Mr. Rabin told you—on the first floor, at the head of a steep stairway. . . ."

"Yes, where you had your accident. He described it to me."

"It was not an accident." The woman sat up. "From behind, she pushed me."

Was she crazy? "Your sister . . . ?"

"Please think, Miss Gaza, as I have thought—now that you know. She was with me, we were going shopping. I was pushed, violently, from behind." And now, finally, there were tears. She took a handkerchief from a pocket of the blue blouse, dabbed at her eyes, returned the handkerchief, closed her eyes for a moment, shook her head, smiled briefly, opened her eyes. "I have a bad history: could I have *imagined* I was pushed? Then I have questions—and answers. If it was an accident, then where was she when I was found at the bottom of the stairs? I am told I was alone. Remember, she was with me. If it was an accident, then where was she when I was taken to the hospital? I am told I was there alone." She lay back, resting her head, the eyes half-closed again. "No, when I recovered, able to think, I knew. They had fooled me there in her apartment; he was not just a casual man, a former employer. Love, Miss Gaza; you're a woman, you know. To protect her lover, my sister tried to kill me—that's the only way any of it made sense. I thought about it for hours lying here in bed: it was the only way it made sense. And I decided. I would not talk. Not fear, Miss Gaza. Not fear that when they learned I was alive they would try to kill me again, no. Quite simply I decided to let her have him. She loved him that much that she was willing to kill for him; let her have him. Mine was not a personal animus against Konrad Kassel; what could I accomplish by telling about him? Vengeance for mass murders so long ago? Let her have him. I decided not to talk."

"Konrad the Fox. We can't prove it yet, but we're quite certain he killed her."

"Will that make the vengeance any better, because it is now personal? I can—and will now and will in the future in any court—tell of Konrad Kassel the murderer. Will that make the vengeance any sweeter because I have condemned the man who murdered my sister who tried to murder me? All vengeance is empty."

"We don't live in a jungle. There are laws. There must be justice."

"Yes."

The sun was hotter. Juliette Gaza felt the taste of perspiration like salt on her lips. "Are you comfortable, Anna?"

"Yes."

"Would you rather go in?"

"No, I am comfortable. Unless you . . . ?"

"Fine, I'm perfectly fine. Anna, just to clear a few matters in your mind. About fear; that anyone would try to kill you, make any attempt again. Mr. Rabin is a wise man. When he learned of your accident, he put two and two together and took no chances. Since it had happened so soon after your visit to the consulate he considered the possibility that it *was* a murder attempt. You were brought here quite secretly and then he engineered a little coup. He planted an item in the newspapers that you had died as a result of your injuries; thus, if it was an attempt the murderer was on notice of its success. During the police investigation of your sister's death, Mr. Rabin informed the police that the newspaper item had been erroneous, that you were alive but still ill here at his home. All of that is confidential, none of it is public knowledge. Now this other thing, your deduction that Gertrude and Mannheim were lovers: you were absolutely correct. Our investigation has disclosed that fact. So—your refusal to speak, at least it was based on valid reason."

"Miss Gaza, if my sister were alive, I would continue that refusal. I had made up my mind. I would not speak."

"Perhaps in its way that's commendable; perhaps in consideration of the full situation, it isn't. Not for me to say." She shrugged. "But now, if you please, to the matter at hand. Anna, we know a great deal about Konrad the Fox, all of it bewildering. We know that in the two months that he was commander of Camp Number Six, sixty thousand human beings were transported from his camp to the ovens at Birkenau, yet at Nuremberg he was not only acquitted, he was adjudged in a sense a humanitarian. He had murdered his own father in outrage, in protection of three Jews whom the father was about to murder outright—four, in fact; you were somewhere about—and these Jews, certainly not Nazi lovers, testified in his defense and buttressed his testimony that he knew nothing of the mass murders, that he was in charge of a labor camp, not a murder camp, that he had supervised transfers from his camp to Birkenau to supplement the labor force at Birkenau, not to stuff its ovens. He admitted he knew about the ovens but insisted that all he knew was that they were for the purpose of cremating the dead—not the living. He insisted that in a vast camp wherein millions of prisoners were held, many died—of dysentery, malnutrition, tuberculosis, many ills—and that the dead, as a matter of health, were cremated. SS Colonel Konrad Kassel was acquitted, and to this day not a shred of evidence has turned up to prove that acquittal an error. Now we have had word from one Anna Stryker—and I'm talking for the record, for the tape recorder taking down our words. Anna Stryker informed the American consulate of Israel here in New York that she had proof of SS Colonel Konrad Kassel's complicity in the mass murders of Auschwitz. If Anna Stryker has such proof, it is our sworn duty to apprehend Konrad Kassel and have him face that proof before a lawfully constituted tribunal. If Anna Stryker does *not* have proof—if her unsworn declarations here and now before me, Juliette Gaza, are comprised of hearsay, conjecture, or evidence inadmissible as testimony in a court of law—then I am empowered by my government to offer its thanks to Anna Stryker for good intentions, to call off any inquiry on behalf of my government as to the whereabouts of Konrad Kassel known in the United States as Konrad Mannheim, and to abstain from any interference in whatever his present activities. There that's done." Juliette Gaza issued a deep sigh, smiled. "So much for the legalistics. And now if you please, Anna. . . ."

"Please, a drink," the woman said. "Would you, please?" A hand outstretched, the fingers moving. Juliette Gaza stood up, went around, but the woman stopped her. "No, please. Not the brandy. The other. I—perhaps I can manage myself."

"You stay right where you are," Juliette Gaza said. She poured iced tea into a glass, gave it to the outstretched hand.

"Thank you." The woman drank thirstily. "Sweet," she said. The great dark eyes were filled with a terror. "I like it sweet," she said. The eyes were somewhere else, the words were here. It was as though, somehow, she was trying to effect a balance. "I like it with lemon but very sweet," she said. "Aliza makes it just the way I like it." A little laugh. There was a tinge of hysteria.

"Are you all right?"

Again the little laugh. "Miss Gaza, you look worried."

"Did I bore you with all that long, legalistic nonsense?"

"Metabolism," the woman said. "The chemistry, the way you burn it up. I never gain weight. Some of us are lucky." She drank again, gave back the empty glass. "Thank you." Juliette Gaza put the glass on the table, pulled her chair nearer, sat, arranged her skirt, and the woman pumped a lever of the lounge chair. Its back moved up until it was almost vertical and she released the lever and now she was fully sitting, her torso at right angles to her thighs and legs. "Yes, I'm ready," she said. She was smiling but it was bad. The lips were smiling but not the eyes and the lines from the nostrils to the edges of the mouth were crevices of perspiration.

"Two ways," Juliette Gaza said brightly. "There are two ways to do this sort of thing. I can prompt you with questions and you answer, or you can have it all to yourself."

"Myself."

"Fine."

"But—I—I won't be able to look at you."

"I'll shift my chair."

"No, no, no—I'd prefer *not* to look."

"Fine," Juliette Gaza said brightly. "Look wherever you like. I'll go away, if you prefer." And once again she pointed to her handbag. "But just talk loud enough, so that thing in there can hear you."

"May I—have it?"

"Pardon?"

"May I have it in my hands? Talk directly to it?"

"Sure," Juliette Gaza said brightly. She opened the bag, took out the recorder, gave it across to Anna Stryker. It was tiny, lightweight, a shiny little object. "Just don't touch any of the little buttons."

"I won't."

Almost fondly the woman held it cupped in her hands. She seemed fascinated, the sunlight glinting off its edges. She kept looking at it, her chin down, her lashes veiling her half-closed eyes, the tip of her tongue visible between parted lips, the shoulders swaying slightly to some internal rhythm of her own, and then the tongue was out of the mouth, licking at the lips, saliva glistening, and then the lips writhed one against the other as though in exercise against a difficulty in speech, but when finally she spoke, although the tone was flat and monotonous, the soft voice was clear, contained, restrained, distinct. . . .

ॐ Twenty-eight

I AM Anna Stryker. I was Mrs. Hermann Koblentz. I am Anna Stryker. My husband is dead. My husband was a good man. I loved and respected him. He was a German. Not a Jew. My husband was a German but never a Nazi. He was born in Dresden. He was an economist. In the post-war Germany he was a high official in the government. During the war he was an officer in the German army. He was a frail man. He suffered. After the war he was a high official in the German government. His health was not good. He came to Sydney in Australia because the doctors advised him. He was told that the climate in Australia would be better for his health. He was respected in Australia just as in Germany. He was a professor in the university when I met him.

I met my husband as a result of a *shidach*. He was a widower. There had been no children in his marriage. I was fifteen years younger than my husband. When I married him I was twenty-nine years old, my sister was twenty-four. By then my grandparents were dead, and my mother a long time before, and my father was dead also a long time. I was living with my sister, or should I say my sister was living with me.

The *shidach*—which is a matrimonial match—was arranged by older people, people who had been friends of my grandparents. It was difficult for me to meet young men, I was very shy. My English was not the best; it still is not the best although it is very much better. One must remember that I spoke only German until I was eleven years old, and from the time I was eleven until sixteen I was in a hospital, a sanitorium, a mental clinic. There I was treated by doctors who spoke German. Thus I did not even begin to learn English until I was sixteen. When I say I spoke only German, it is not quite accurate. I also spoke Yiddish, and some of my doctors in the sanitorium also spoke Yiddish.

When the *shidach* was broached to me, I was reluctant. But this old lady who had been a friend of my grandmother said, "Anna, it is time. It is not healthy for a girl to stay so long unmarried."

When I state what people said, it is not exact but it is substantially what they said.

And the old man who was her husband said, "A very fine person. Herr Doktor Koblentz, a professor in the university. Once an important man with the government in the homeland, but here he is a lonely person and you will make him a good wife."

"He knows about me?" I asked.

The old woman understood what I meant and I remember how she bobbed her head. "Everything," she said. "He knows all about you—all, everything."

It was a happy marriage. He was not a well man—lung trouble—which he told me before we got married. We invited my sister to live with us, which she accepted. In my marriage I did not have children. My only blood relative was my sister.

My husband was a quiet man, a good man and kind. It seems he made a point not to talk about Germany, his experiences or mine, nor about my time in the sanitorium except if I would bring it up and then the conversation, because he knew it could be painful, would be brief.

The sanitorium. I was there five years. Five years is a long time but now it does not seem to be so long at all. It was—how shall I say?—a long cure. For almost two years I did not speak at all, I did not say a single word. And then slowly—very slowly—did I return to life.

I was sick when I arrived in Australia, withdrawn, already not speaking. My good grandparents brought me to the sanitorium for what they hoped would be a short period of cure. Five years. But one must try to understand the extent of my illness, one must try to understand the effects upon a child of . . . well . . . not being out in the sun, not once, from the time she was about five years old until she was eleven. One must understand the constant dread, the whispers, the fright. One must understand the conditions of being hidden, the closeness, the lack of any recreation, the lack of food, the lack of privacy even for the most intimate bodily functions.

I was born in Dresden and we were hidden by the Germans of Dresden. In time they themselves did not have enough food; we, the hidden Jews, were always hungry. Some of our group did not survive. There were times a body remained with us until it rotted. Even now I can remember the stench. . . .

We were always somewhere in a basement. From time to time, at night, we were transferred, those of us still alive. But always to another basement. In the summer we burned of heat. In the winter we shivered of cold. I had painful sores on my body. There was never a toilet. One corner of the basement would be the place to go. When one went, the others turned their heads. There was always the stench. And in all those years I never once saw the sun.

Long before, at the beginning, my mother and baby sister were taken by the underground out of the country. They went with many others, but only two from a family. I remained behind with my father. When we heard, almost a year later through the grapevine, we learned that my mother had died on the way but that my sister was safe with my grandparents, the mother and father of my mother, in Australia.

When I saw the sun I was eleven years old. We were taken out by soldiers in uniform. There were only four of us left—my father and me, Alfred Holzer, and Benjamin Jankowski. We knew—the grapevine—that the war was practically at an end. But not for us. With others, standing, packed in a freight car, we were shipped to Auschwitz. Camp Number Six. The commandant was SS Colonel Konrad Kassel. I remember my father with Mr. Jankowski and Mr. Holzer—while I clung to my father's hand—pleading with Colonel Kassel for the lives of the Jews of Auschwitz. What sense the further killings, the further murders—ours included? The war was at end.

I remember Colonel Konrad Kassel, tall and straight and young. He denied there had ever been murders of Jews. He admitted he was the commandant of only one small camp, Camp Number Six, and that he had only been there two months. But he offered to take us the next day to Birkenau, to the man second in command of the entire concentration camp, SS General Wilhelm von Kassel, his own father.

"I am not really the one to speak to," he said. "I am not a warden of political prisoners, I am a soldier. I have been with the Luftwaffe, served my time, and now they have transferred me here, but my father has been at Auschwitz since the beginning. He will tell you. He will convince you. Jews! You enjoy to live under a myth of persecution. You are enemies of the State, and as such you are detained in our camps and do labor as prisoners. But nobody is murdering you, nobody is killing you. A myth. I shall bring you to General von Kassel, and you will have proof. You will be convinced."

The next day we were taken in an Army motorcar, a soldier was driving. I remember we were sitting in the back of the motorcar, Mr. Jankowski, Mr. Holzer, my father, me, and Colonel Kassel—and that was all I was able to remember. I could remember nothing else. Nothing. . . .

In the sanitorium, after I was able to talk, I could remember everything up to that point—in the motorcar with my father and the others—and nothing else. And I never *did* remember. After five years when I was released as cured—I still did not remember. The doctors told me it was not of any great matter—a block in my mind which did not at all interfere with my cure. Some day, possibly, I would remember, but it would make no difference in my condition. Simply, if I remembered then I remembered, it would fill in a blank; nevertheless I was cured. I heard later about the testimony my father had given, and Mr. Jankowski, and Mr. Holzer, and that Colonel Konrad Kassel had been acquitted at Nuremberg, but frankly it did not interest me; five years had passed and I was beginning a new life.

My grandparents were very good to me. They were not poor.

154

They gave me private tutors and sent me to private school. And as I said, in time I got married and I was very happily married. . . .

It was about two and a half years ago that my husband fell badly ill. The lungs. With hemorrhage. He was six months in the hospital. It was when he came home that my sister went to America, about two years ago. Last year, my husband died. I went back to work. Before I was married, I used to work in a library. I took back my maiden name—Anna Stryker—and went back to work in the library, but it was not good. I was finished in Australia. I decided to move, to go to Israel and live there the rest of my life. My husband had left money—a policy and a small personal estate. There was enough, sufficient. I made my arrangements. Passport, visas, everything, all in order. I would have a six-month visit in America, and then to Israel. My sister had obtained for me, before I came, the furnished apartment here in New York, and I arrived, it must be now two weeks. She was most pleasant with me, gave me much of her time. She showed me the city, we shopped. She visited with me, and I with her. And then it was Thursday, this Thursday. I was in her apartment in Flushing, Borough of Queens. The bell rang, and the man came. Konrad Mannheim, she told me. Konrad Mannheim of Mannheim Incorporated where she had worked, formerly her boss. He was the same, straight and tall and not much changed, SS Colonel Konrad Kassel. And seeing him, suddenly I remembered. All! They had told me it could happen. Suddenly. A touch, a sight, a smell, something. It could trigger. That was the word, an expression—trigger. Suddenly, trigger, a release, possible, it could happen. After all tne many years I saw him in my sister's apartment in Flushing in the Borough of Queens. In New York. United States. America. Suddenly. . . .

The motorcar. It goes swiftly. It is a dark day, a cloudy day. I tremble in the rear of the motorcar, near my father. He scarcely knows I am even near. It is a mission. My father, Jankowski, Holzer, and the straight-backed awesome man in the visored cap and uniform.

A stone house, a white stone house. The motorcar stops. Soldiers salute. We go in, led by Colonel Konrad Kassel. We are in a room, vast, bare, only wooden benches. The colonel goes away. My father is deeply talking to Mr. Jankowski and Mr. Holzer.

Nobody pays attention to me. I wander off. A door. I open it, go through. Corridors. I walk along corridors, there are many doors. I open a door. It is a great big room, also with many doors. It has many desks, many chairs. There are flags on the walls, and maps of many colors. I hear sounds, footsteps coming. I rush under one of the huge desks, crouching. The back of the desk is perforated, a grillwork. I can see through.

The colonel enters with a man as tall as he, but an old man. The old man, in a resplendent uniform, takes off his visored cap, lays it on a desk. He has white hair and a white mustache, its ends turned up. A splendid man, a frightening man.

"You have arranged it?" the old man says.

"Yes, Father," the colonel says.

"It is the only way," the old man says. "It will save your life."

"I don't know if I can go through with it," the colonel says.

"You *will!*" The old man has a harsh voice, a commanding voice. "I am dead," the old man says, "I am already dead, there has been a final diagnosis. It is cancer of the liver, and has passed into the body. There cannot be an operation, there can only be a few months of suffering. If you don't, then I do. A bullet in the head. But you *must*, it will save your life. They will be present, they will see, you will be their hero. You have told them you know nothing? There have been no killings of the damned Jews? You will prove it by this interview with your father?"

"I have told them," the colonel says.

"All arranged as we have arranged it?" the old man says.

"Entirely arranged," the colonel says.

"I am glad I am going to die," the old man says. "The war is at a close. It is over. Our plans, our dreams—vanquished. Already the great ones are fleeing, and even from here I have released the major contingent of my personal staff and the guards. Let them flee. For me there now is death and for you—life. It is our moment, my son. We are virtually alone, you and I and the damn Jews you have brought—but they will be your salvation. Do you love Jews?" The old man laughs.

"I hate Jews," the colonel says.

"Well, these Jews you must love," the old man says, "and they will love you and they will *save* you, the ignorant swine."

"I will try," the colonel says.

"Exactly as we prepared, as arranged?" the old man says.

"Exactly. I will try," the colonel says.

"You know nothing of liquidation, of final solution. You are a flyer in the Luftwaffe, a fighting soldier." Again the old man laughs. "You are an innocent in politics, an ignorant, as ignorant as they."

"I want them dead, dead as all the others, all of them, the last of them," the colonel says.

"Not these," the old man says. "These we keep alive—to give life to you. These are your pawns. Now bring them in. And—exactly as we arranged." The old man puts on his visored cap.

They embrace. They kiss. The colonel goes out quickly and quickly marches back my father, Mr. Janowski, and Mr. Holzer.

"General von Kassel," the colonel says and clicks his heels.

"My child, my daughter," my father says. "She has wandered off, lost here somewhere. . . ."

"We are not interested in your damn child. . . ." The tall old man in his resplendent uniform confronts my father. "Now what in hell do you want here?"

But it was Mr. Holzer who spoke, his plea for the Jews of Auschwitz cut off by a shout from the colonel to his father. "Tell them we Germans are not wild animals . . . we have removed the Jews from our society . . . imprisoned them in camps . . . but we are not wild animals in a jungle . . . we do not kill defenseless humans. . . ."

"Humans!" And now it was the old man, General von Kassel, shouting at his son, and he marched to my father and slapped his face and with the back of his hand slapped Holzer and then with a fist struck Jankowski. "My son is a fool, an innocent!" And he faced the colonel. "Jews, vile . . . sub-human . . . war is over . . . contingents will be here this very day . . . but our work does not stop . . . these dirty specimens . . . I myself will have the pleasure. . . ."

The old man pulled his pistol.

"No!" the colonel shouted at him, and he himself pulled out his pistol.

"Fool!" the old man spat at his son. "Stand away." He aimed his pistol at Mr. Holzer.

Then Colonel Kassel shot his father. I can smell the smoke right now. I can see the blood right now, and the smash of the old man's head, and I can hear the thump of his body as it fell, and I ran out from my hiding place and ran screaming to my father and right now I can hear myself screaming.

I can hear my screams. . . .

℘ Twenty-nine

JULIETTE GAZA took the recorder from the stiff fingers of the woman in the lounge chair. She switched off the recording device, returned the instrument to her bag. The woman's eyes were closed, her lips caked, tiny bubbles of white spittle-like foam at the corners of her mouth.

"Anna."

The woman's eyes opened. She smiled. She took the handkerchief from the pocket of the blouse, wiped her mouth, opened the handkerchief, refolded it, dabbed at her eyes, patted her lips, carefully adjusted the handkerchief in the pocket of the blue blouse. Juliette Gaza stood up and went around to the table on the other side and picked up the glasses of brandy Rabin had poured for them (it seemed so long ago). She offered one to Anna who, this time, accepted.

"Thank you."

Juliette Gaza, tired of sitting, preferred to stand, but that would put a strain on the woman in the lounge chair who would be compelled to look up, so she went back to her chair, sat, sipped. The brandy, warm from the sun, was fruity. But good.

"Anna, this in a way is a personal question."

"Yes, Miss Gaza?"

"You took back your maiden name . . . ?"

The woman smiled. "I would expect you would ask that question." A sip of the brandy. "Prejudice, we all have prejudice. While my husband was alive. . . ." Another sip of brandy and again the little smile. "You know—I mentioned?—he was from Dresden. It was one basis for the *shidach*. The old people who arranged the match, they had known relatives of his. We were, my husband and I, in a way, townsfolk, *landsmann*. But when he died, when I was alone again, I could not live with that name, so German—Mrs. Hermann Koblentz. It was not Anna Stryker, you know? Once he was dead I was not, simply not, a Mrs. Hermann Koblentz. Please. You understand?"

"If not I—who?"

"Thank you, Miss Gaza."

"Anna, just a few little things now and I won't bore you with me any more."

"Please not." The black eyes with humor. "You do not bore me, Miss Gaza."

"Anna, about Mr. Mannheim, your Colonel Konrad Kassel. To begin—when the police come. They'll come—how long can Rabin hold them off?—about . . . Gertrude Stryker. You will tell the truth, except where it can interfere with us. There must not be mention of any suspicion that your sister attacked you. . . ."

"No, of course not!"

"And not a single word about Mr. Konrad Mannheim of Mannheim Incorporated; not from you, Anna. Checking back on her they'll come to him, but merely as a former employer, what else? Nothing from you. Nothing that you know. We don't want interference from local police. We must keep him out of their waters. He is a large fish for *us* to fry."

"Yes, I understand."

Juliette Gaza, already feeling the flush of the warm brandy, finished what was in the glass and put the glass aside on the table. "Anna, we're searching for him and we have reason to believe we'll catch up with him in short order. But *we* want him, rather than the local police; yes?"

"Yes."

"Now we have you, and so we have him. With you as witness —your testimony—Konrad the Fox who so long bewildered us will finally stand trial." She picked up her glass, saw it was empty, put it down. "He is an important man now, Anna, far more important than the youthful Colonel Kassel of Camp Number Six at Auschwitz. The world turns, moves: Konrad Kassel is right now being molded—by great powers, great influences, great money—into a political figure of international stature. He is on his way to Germany and once there *we* will never have him again. Power, influence, money will twist the tables against us; protect him and defeat us; make a hero of him again; better yet, a martyr pursued and persecuted by destructive, vicious, present-day remnants of the old order of racial enmity and hatred. In Germany—backed by power, money, lawyers, politics—he will emerge as a triumphant world figure; or, the powers behind him possibly convinced they cannot thwart our proof, then he will be submerged and disappear and our long, painful search will commence again, and all dependent upon you, your life span; only you, Anna; the only witness who can personally testify. Do you understand?"

A sip of the brandy, and the glass placed away on her table.

"A little. Not all. It is . . . too much for me."

"And for me, Anna. Who are we? Little people. We do what we think right, we contribute our little share. There are others, bigger, greater, more learned, who know how to fix in our little contributions in the complex mosaic of world affairs." That was very good, that last; she was rather proud the way she had put it. She attempted a tremulous little sigh to punctuate it, but the sigh came out real, deep and despairing. Juliette Gaza desired more brandy but was ashamed to get up and get it. "Anna," she said, "when we get him, we won't let him."

"What?" asked Anna Stryker.

"Anna," she said, and laughed, "it won't cost you. Transportation to Israel for free. There's a plane waiting, government plane. They know where to take you and there are people in Israel ready, willing, able, and anxious to take care of you. You will go when we ask?"

"Ask?"

"When we are ready to take you?"

"Yes."

"It can be sudden."

"Yes."

"There's another of us here."

"Another?"

"From Shinbet. Dave Jordan. Mr. Rabin knows him. You'll meet him."

"Yes."

"That's about all of it, Anna. Thank you."

"For what?"

"For—what?"

"For what do you thank me?"

"All . . . everything. . . ."

"I thank you, Miss Gaza."

℞ Thirty

AFTERNOON of the fourth day. Four days now, McGregor waiting. Nine to three. Lincoln National Bank. Madison Avenue at 44th Street. Nine to three without eating. A kind of diet. A solid breakfast, then the nine to three gap, then home for a bite and a nap, then dinner with Tillie. Nine to three, a long vigil, but not boring. Carefully, craftily, shifting from car to cab, from cab to car, but constantly alert. Expectant. Watching Juliette Gaza's man watching for Konrad Mannheim. Each day but at uncertain hours—the lady must have other matters to attend—she joins her man in the watch for Mannheim. She drives a station wagon, slowly circling the block. Check on station wagon: property of Mrs. Gideon Rabin.

Afternoon of the fourth day, cloudy and cool. McGregor in the rear of a limousine, the driver Joe Carter, a bright young cop in plain clothes. McGregor checks his watch. Five minutes after two. And there she goes again disappearing around the corner, Juliette Gaza circling in the station wagon. The fiancé—fiancé?—there he stands now across the street in the entranceway of an office building. Knows his business, the fiancé. Keeps loose. Never loiters long in one spot. There he stands now, unobtrusive. Good figure of a man. Tall and slim but wide at the shoulders, and very nicely dressed today. Black shoes, black trousers with a sharp crease, a natty raglan topcoat with fashionable patch pockets. One fashionable patch pocket, the fashionable patch pocket on the right side, loses a bit of its style because of the bulge. Nothing inordinate, but if you look hard enough, a good-size bulge. Well, naturally. This guy's no dope: if you're going to carry artillery, well then the hell let it be an effective piece. Simple logistics. A matter of firepower. If you assume the other guy is braced by a .22, then if you double the firepower you figure to have twice the advantage in the event the sports and games degenerate to combat.

McGregor yawns.

Afternoon in New York City.

Business area. Teeming streets, crowded sidewalks.

Commences another yawn and it gets stuck. Fights off lockjaw, peers. The cab at the curb by the bank deposits a passenger. Nerves prick at McGregor's scalp like a network of needles. Konrad Mannheim, jaunty in a Tyrolean hat and carrying a compact plaid-patterned suitcase, enters into the Lincoln National Bank.

Immediately the man in the raglan coat crosses the street.

"We're with it, Joe," McGregor says.

"Come again, Inspector?"

"Start her up. Quick now."

"Yessir, Inspector."

Joe Carter touches the ignition. The motor turns over.

"Keep her at idle."

"Yessir, Inspector."

The man in the raglan coat has his eye out for the station wagon and when it comes he flags it. He talks to the woman at the wheel, goes back near the entrance to the bank. The station wagon remains double-parked by the bank.

"Joe."

"Yessir, Inspector?"

"See the wagon there by the bank? With the chick at the wheel?"

"Yes."

"The guy with the coat with the patch pockets? Over there?"

"Yes."

"Did you notice the guy with the Tyrolean hat?"

162

"No."

"Went into the bank?"

"No."

"Okay, listen hard now, lad. In case we have to split, you tail the station wagon. Use your talkie. Don't be bashful. Keep talking to the talkie, reporting to Headquarters. You got that?"

"Yessir, Inspector. But in case we don't split?"

"Then what the hell would you have to worry about?"

A pause. A chuckle. "Yeah, you got a point there, Inspector."

"Keep her at idle, but keep her ready to go."

"Yessir, Inspector."

McGregor waits, muscles tense, legs and shoulders aching, the limousine a prison. By the bank the man in the raglan coat is also waiting, his right hand sunk deep in the right-hand pocket of the coat. McGregor snaps a glance at the station wagon. Fumes from the exhaust show the motor is churning.

Konrad Mannheim now. Tall and jaunty, emerging from the bank. Carrying the plaid suitcase without visible effort. (How much do a thousand thousand-dollar bills weigh?) And is immediately accosted by the man in the raglan coat. His left arm links with Mannheim's right arm, the plaid bag between them. Quick talk, quick movement. Toward the station wagon. Juliette Gaza, leaning over, opens the passenger door. Mannheim, urged by a tug at his arm, gets in. Followed by the man in the raglan coat. The door shuts. The station wagon moves.

"Go, Joe. Don't lose them."

"Don't worry, Inspector."

Konrad Mannheim, the bag on his knees, sat quietly between the woman on his left and the man on his right. The man's pistol was now out of his pocket, a huge revolver, held in his lap on the folds of his coat.

"So far so good," the man said. "But don't even *think* of trying anything funny, Mr. Mannheim, or you wind up a very dead bastard. Is that clear? Or would you like it translated to German?"

"It is clear."

"Good boy."

He had no intention of trying anything funny or unfunny. He would try, in time, to talk them out of it, or out of a part of it,

163

but was already resigned to losing it all. Robbery, well-planned; he had to admire. They knew his name and as evidenced by the sarcastic remark, even his ethnic origin. Lubeck—who else? Somewhere along the line, somehow, however innocently, Lubeck had opened his foolish mouth, and that gave these bandits a full protection. Can a thief go to the police to complain about the stealing of his stolen loot? How did the Americans call it?— hijacking. But what they knew—their very knowledge—would serve to preserve his life. Since he was powerless to bring formal complaint, they would not complicate a successful robbery by the irreversible crime of murder. No, my dear sir, nothing funny or unfunny. He was and would continue to be, docile—to the tune of a million dollars. It hurt, oh it hurt, it was ashes in his mouth, but his life, at this stage of his life, was all important, was worth the forfeit of a million dollars, or many millions of dollars. No, my dear sir, I do not wish to wind up a very dead bastard. Not at this time of my life; there are great plans being built up around me. Put away your big, gleaming revolver. Don't be nervous, I am docile. I concede. I know the meaning and value of compromise. You win, I lose, but however it hurts it is a minor battle in my war. Nothing funny or unfunny, my dear sir, I promise you.

The woman drove smoothly. A turn, a stop at a red light, another turn, and they were going north on Park Avenue where the traffic was less dense. Then another turn and they were at the Delmonico Hotel.

"Dave, you take him up."

"Right."

"I'll get parked. Be with you shortly."

"Right."

"Be good, Mr. Mannheim. Don't make Dave rough."

"Yes," he said.

Delmonico. McGregor watching. The raglan coat and the Tyrolean hat. Out of the wagon and into the hotel, they go together. The lady parks the car. Then carrying the plaid suitcase, she is swallowed into the hotel.

"Joe, you carrying your piece?"

"Regulations. I got to."

"You good at shooting, Joe?"

"I got a marksman's medal, Inspector."

"Take it out and lay it alongside you. On the seat."

"We gonna have action?"

"Could be."

"Now?"

"Not now. Maybe later. Out and on the seat, Joe."

"Yessir, Inspector."

Juliette Gaza knocked on the door of 1400. Dave Jordan opened the door, closed it behind her and locked it, returned her key. She set down the plaid suitcase, dropped the key in her bag, snapped it shut, smiled at Konrad Mannheim, admired his poise. Cool was the modern expression for it. She admired his cool.

He was seated in an armchair by a window, his legs crossed, his Tyrolean hat on the floor beside him, his fingertips touched together in a horizontal pyramid in his lap, the heels of his hands against his belly. She was almost tempted to offer him a drink.

"Get up," she said.

He stood up, quite gracefully.

Dave covered him with the revolver.

"If you please," Mannheim said, "I know when I am defeated." The *cool* of the son of a bitch. "I offer," he said and smiled, "a token of my surrender."

"Like what?" Dave said.

"In my pocket, a pistol. I surrender it."

"Brother, you make one wrong move. . . ."

"I will not move." He put his hands in the air. "Please, if the lady will come and take it. My token of surrender."

She went to him quickly, touched him all over for weapons, found only that one, a .22, remembered what McGregor had told them about Gertrude Stryker, and put away the .22 into her handbag. If she could help the local police in the solution of a local murder, why not?

"If you please," Mannheim said. "If I may make a suggestion."

"What?" Dave said.

"Ill gotten gains by ill gotten means." The man smiled. "I suggest—compromise. An intelligent negotiation between respected adversaries. And without recrimination. Honor, as they say, among. . . ." The planes of his face descended as the smile abruptly ceased. "I suggest—a split. Fifty-fifty. Divided, it still makes an enormous sum. No recriminations. We divide, and go our separate ways. We maintain our respect, and we restrain hatred and smouldering remnants of ultimate vengeance. I do respect what you have accomplished—please respect what I have. And on that note of respect—compromise. There is enough. We divide and go our separate ways, each with respect."

"No," Dave said.

Mannheim glanced toward her and then back to Dave. "Yes of course, I ask the lady's pardon. I have lumped you, I ask your pardon. We are three. Still there is enough. Divided by three, still each sum is enormous. The basis of negotiation, my plea to you—no recrimination, no harboring of hatred, respect one for the other. Respect. Mutual respect for accomplishment, division of spoils, and we go our separate ways. Honor among. What say? Vanquished, it is my offer. There is enough for all. Without hatred and with respect. No recriminations."

Dave Jordan looked toward her and she nodded. He spun the revolver by its trigger-guard, reversing it in his hand. "Well," he said and approached Mannheim. Expertly he swung the butt at Mannheim's chin and the man fell forward on his knees like a stricken bull at the moment of truth, then his body turned and he was flat on his back, arms outstretched.

"Do we tie him up?"

"No need. Take off his jacket. Roll up a shirtsleeve."

"Yes ma'am. You're the boss."

She disappeared into a bedroom, came back with a small plastic-wrapped package. "Squeeze tight over the elbow. No. Use both hands. Yes, that's it. I need a stick-out vein. You're the tourniquet. Very good. Just like that. Hold it." She tore at the plastic with her teeth, ripped open the package, extracted a slender syrette. "Sterile. Absolutely sterile." The needle punctured the protruding vein. She eased it in, applied a gradual pressure on the plunger. "There," she said, tossed away the empty syrette. "He'll have a peaceful sleep."

"How long does it last?"

"About eighteen hours."

Now Jordan was at the plaid suitcase. Locked. He took keys from Mannheim's jacket, opened the suitcase.

"Holy Jesus Christ! Something?"

She looked. "A bonus to the State of Israel from the National Socialist League of Argentina, but we have the real prize." Went to her bag, gave him a key. "You know the trunk. Take him. Strap him in carefully." And as he moved to comply. "Wait a minute. His jacket, everything. His hat."

"Okay, Boss. You're the boss."

And while he labored, she called Rabin. And when he came back she was saying, ". . . yes, that's it exactly. Thank you, sir. Goodbye for now." She hung up.

"Procedure?" he said.

"I'm about to call the porter for the trunk."

"His suitcase?"

"You'll take it."

"The other trunks?"

"They're staying."

"You're remaining?"

"Yes, for a few days. Things to do, clean up. I'll be going by regular commercial airline. You won't have any trouble, Dave, nothing, none at all. Diplomatic clearance, the trunk, the suitcase, reciprocal agreements, right now Mr. Rabin is making sure. You'll go right through, and the crew of our jet knows exactly where to take you—you and Anna Stryker."

"Rabin? He'll see me through to the plane?"

"No. I don't want him that closely involved. His job is the outside job, normal diplomatic job. You and I, Dave, we're inside." She grinned. "We're the commandos. Anything goes wrong, it's our brunt."

"Right."

"You'll pick up Anna Stryker. She'll be ready. Then direct to the airport. Leave the wagon, don't worry about the station wagon. It's all smooth for you, Dave. We've done it. Go and God bless. See you in Tel Aviv."

McGregor and Joe Carter. Waiting. Watching. The man in the raglan coat carrying the plaid suitcase. Goes quickly to the station wagon. Heaves in the suitcase, drives the station wagon to the hotel. A porter, using a hand truck, rolls out a trunk. Raglan coat supervises as the trunk is deposited in the rear of the station wagon. Tips the porter, drives off.

"Stay with him, Joe."

"You bet, Inspector."

"He's still got his bulge."

"Beg pardon?"

"Artillery. In his right-hand coat pocket."

"Oh."

"Where's yours?"

"Right here on the seat."

"Good lad."

North, then east. The wagon stops at a tall apartment house on 70th Street. Outside, a pile of luggage guarded by a man in a chauffeur's uniform, and near him a small dark woman with a strip of adhesive on her forehead, and an older woman whom McGregor recognizes, Aliza Rabin. A honk from the wagon and they all come alive. The driver gets out of the wagon. Assists the man in the chauffeur's uniform. Luggage in. Rear of the wagon closed. The women kiss. The dark woman gets in beside the driver. The door slams. The wagon moves off.

"I had hoped Miss Gaza would be able to make the trip with me."

"She's still got things to do back here."

The woman sighed. "I know. She told me. But I'd hoped."

"A lot of those things have got to do with you. You know, your sister. . . ."

"Yes, I know, Mr. Jordan."

Silence.

"Change of weather," he said.

"Yes."

"Looked like rain before. But it's all cleared up. And getting real warm."

"Yes."

And that was it. Not another word from her all the way to the airport. Damn silent woman. Sure, he was a stranger. Only met

168

her the other evening. So what? People talk, strangers. Well, just as good. Who needs it with conversation? And slid a glance toward her. Eyes closed. As though asleep. A shy one. Or some kind of goddamn snob. Who cares either way? The hell with you, lady.

And drove. Carefully. Steadily. Watching speed.

And arrived. Kennedy International.

Ah, the power of the damn diplomats. Not a single hitch. Smooth as silk. Everybody practically bowing and scraping. And then out on the airfield. Huge jet. Competent crew. Taking over. First the trunk with Mannheim. Swallowed in. Then Anna Stryker's luggage. Then Anna Stryker. Swallowed in. A short conversation with the pilot. Hearty handshake. Good luck. The pilot is swallowed in. The jet closes, taxies away. He waves with his left hand, his right hand holding the plaid suitcase. Turns away from the wind and the roar. And is jostled. McGregor on his right side. A tall young man on his left. McGregor's hand clamps his hand holding the suitcase. And the tall young man, smiling, points a pistol.

᠘ Thirty-one

THE rest of the day was all business for Juliette Gaza. She wanted to get as much done as possible as quickly as possible. At 3:30 there was her appointment with Hugh Massey, Anna Stryker's lawyer, at his office. He had obtained all the necessary court orders and the bond. Rabin himself had put up the collateral for the bond. That meant that tomorrow they could withdraw Gertrude Stryker's money from the banks, the bond was firm to cover all eventualities. She wanted to be able to take the cash to Anna Stryker in Israel. But today she would have to go to the Borough of Queens with Hugh Massey to pick up the bank books from the police custodian. There was also the appointment with the auctioneer who was arranging the sale of Gertrude Stryker's belongings. And there was the matter of the balance of McGregor's fee, to which he was now eminently entitled. And the business of Mannheim's .22 pistol which in effect, she was certain, would close the police file on the Gertrude Stryker murder. She would give the gun to McGregor. Let him get the credit. Tit for tat. He had done so much for her: why not she for him? But was that it? No, it was not it, exactly. She wanted him, damn, under obligation to her, because, damn, she wanted him. The damn handsome man, he had become a gnawing ache to her. Juliette Gaza, the modern Mata Hari, hah hah, of the vaunted sex appeal. But with McGregor she had absolutely failed.

Had she?

Certainly the man McGregor was no quick-trick Dave Jordan. This was an intricate man, a damn interesting man. Were those cold blue eyes as unappreciative of her charms as they appeared to be? She refused to believe that.

She called him from the hotel before leaving for Massey's office. No answer. She left her name.

She called him from Massey's office. No answer, left her name again with the answering service.

Called him from the police station in Queens after calling her hotel for messages. No message at the hotel, no answer at his apartment. She left her name.

Later, it was 6:15 and she was back home in 1400, the phone rang and she was certain it was he. It was Aliza Rabin.

"Will you have dinner with us, dear?"

She was hungry. "Well. . . ."

"Please do. A going-out dinner. The Colony. Gideon absolutely insists, and so do I."

"Thank you, yes."

She called McGregor. No answer. Somewhat embarrassedly— all those damn calls—she told the service she would be in the Colony Restaurant until ten o'clock, after that she would be in her suite in the Delmonico Hotel.

She came home to 1400 at 9:15, checked for messages, nothing. Was he dead? She undressed, bathed, perfumed, waited. The call came at precisely 10:30. She was in bed watching TV, naked.

"Miss Gaza?"

"I'm glad you're not dead, Mr. McGregor."

"Alive."

"I called you a million times."

"Got the messages."

"Don't you ever the hell call a person back?"

"Busy. Work. I want to see you, Miss Gaza."

"And I you. Come over."

"No, I'm afraid I must ask you to come to me."

She didn't like her laugh. It was arch, high in the palate, teasing. Nonetheless it was conciliatory. "All right. I'm not one for ceremonial proprieties."

"Beautifully put, Miss Gaza."

"I know where. I'll see you in half an hour."

"No."

"Now what?"

"I'm not home." He gave her an address. "It's a station house, a precinct house. Tell them Homicide. Ask for Lieutenant Louis Parker."

"Oh the hell, Mr. McGregor."

"Necessary, Miss Gaza."

"I believe I've met Lieutenant Parker, if it's the same Lieutenant Parker."

"The same."

"Must I?"

"I believe it best."

Pause. Then. "All right. Half an hour."

"Thank you."

"Welcome."

McGregor hung up.

Parker said, "You slipping, Inspector?"

"Could be. Am I?" He lit a cigarette.

"I didn't hear a goddamn word about a .22."

"Didn't *say* a word about a .22."

171

"What I goddamn mean. What I mean, why not?"

"Do we know she has it?"

Parker bit on his cigar. "Well. . . ."

"Could I make the demand?"

"Hell, you could give a hint."

"Louie, you know whom we're dealing with."

"We're dealing with a goddamn international agent."

"Exactly. And I've already laid it on the line about Mannheim and the .22. If she has it and she wants to cooperate, she will. If not, how do we force it?"

"Yeah, maybe you got something there. Look, I'm not complaining. You closed up my file on Ludwig Lubeck, and you sure brought in the stuff that's going to make me a whole big-chested hero. Hell, the Lubeck, we didn't even know who the hell he was. Now I know it all, and your action in the action—and the action we've been giving it—and I hate to say it, but a lot of it's way over my head. But I kind of promised the Queens guys on the Gertrude Stryker. . . ."

"Louie, intuition. I think she'll bring it in."

"The .22?"

"If he had it on him, and she's got it, I think."

Parker's eyes smiled. "You a little soft on that chick?

"You saw her."

"Oh, that I did."

"A beautiful woman."

"Inspector, from the look of you—I've got a whole big snitch for Tillie."

"Not you, Louie."

"I'm a moral man. Strictly conservative."

"Conservative equals stoolie?"

"Never happened."

"Thank you, Lieutenant."

Grin. "You mean you got intentions?"

"Don't we all, every now and then? Truth, Louie. Have you ever strayed?"

"Inspector, in my humble opinion you're as great a cop as ever was. But a priest for confession you're not."

"Shall we leave it at that, Mr. Parker?"

"We goddamn will, Mr. McGregor."

She combed her hair carefully, dressed carefully, carefully applied her makeup. She made certain to transfer the little gun to the handbag matching her outfit. She thought about the balance of his fee, and decided not to take it. Plenty of cash in the trunk. A ploy to bring him back. Disgusting. As though he would, only for the money. But it *would* provide an excuse. Julie, you're disgusting, and laughed at herself in a mirror. But at least he would know where he was coming, to whom he was coming. That decision had been made even before his phone call. Senseless to further dissimulate. Not with one like him. He had probably known —even before Lieutenant Parker—that she was not a wistful little wife seeking a husband delinquent in alimony. She gave another touch to her hair, and gave herself another smile, a sardonic smile, in the mirror, and went out into a soft, starry night for a cab. Dear God, what a beautiful night. Clear, cloudless, with a warm little breeze and a huge white moon. A romantic night. A night for romance.

Julie, get hold of yourself.

The doorman blew his whistle for a cab.

℞ Thirty-two

SHE was ushered in by a uniformed policeman. McGregor was immediately on his feet. They shook hands. She held his hand a trifle longer than he held hers. She was sure he noticed. Then she turned to the dark man, smiled. "Lieutenant."

He inclined his head. "Miss Gaza."

She opened her bag, took out the little pistol, gave it to McGregor.

"I believe you were interested in this."

"From Mannheim?"

"Yes."

He grinned, gave the pistol to Parker, who gave it to the uniformed policeman.

"Ballistics check on this, Brody."

"Yessir."

"On Gertrude Stryker. The Queens thing. The stuff is here. I want to know right away."

"Yessir, I'll tell them."

Brody went out. The lieutenant smiled at her, motioned to a chair. It was a wooden armchair. There were many chairs in the big room, none soft. The lights were harsh, the blinds on all the windows drawn. It was a clean room, no pictures on the walls. There was a large rectangular desk, uncluttered. It held four phones, one with buttons, and an intercom with many levers. The room had three doors in addition to the one through which she had entered.

She returned the lieutenant's smile but did not accept the chair he indicated. Instead she chose one that faced McGregor's. She sat, crossed her knees, her skirt hiking up. She didn't touch it.

McGregor sat, lit a cigarette. The lieutenant went around to the swivel chair behind his desk.

"Aren't you arranged in districts?" she said.

"Pardon?" The lieutenant frowned.

"I mean—I thought—there were different jurisdictions."

"I don't understand," the lieutenant said.

"I mean—Gertrude Stryker. That's Queens, another district, isn't it? You, here, Lieutenant Parker—that's the city proper. I mean on the ballistics. Wouldn't that be the province of the Queens police?"

The lieutenant, smiling again, said admiringly, "You're something, Miss." Nodded. "Yes, under · normal circumstances, it *would* be the province of the Queens police."

"I butted in," McGregor said, "and made the circumstances abnormal."

"You, Mr. McGregor?"

"Me." The blue eyes smiled. She loved the contrast of the black eyebrows and the white hair. A striking man. "Once I knew you had Mannheim, I hoped you'd get his little pistol to me."

"You knew—"

"Yes. And if you did get it to me, I'd turn it over to Lieutenant

Parker. We've been working together most of the day, the lieutenant and I." He inhaled cigarette smoke. "Which is the reason I couldn't get back to you until late; I mean your phone messages. Anyway, if you did present us with Mannheim's little pistol—which would have the further condition precedent that he had it on him—I didn't intend for us to go dragging all the way out to Queens on what, quite possibly, could turn out to be a fool's errand. Police cooperate. Lieutenant Parker requested copies of the ballistics photographs, and they're here, and the experts are checking. Right now, on this phase, police cooperating, Lieutenant Parker's in charge."

"I see." Time now. "Mr. McGregor, did Lieutenant Parker inform you . . . ?" No. Wrong tack. "Mr. McGregor, about myself. I am not an ex-wife worried about alimony. I was never married to Mr. Mannheim, thank God. I work for the Israeli government, myself an Israeli citizen. Shinbet. You know Shinbet?"

"I know Shinbet." He put out his cigarette in an ashtray.

"My job was Mannheim. This of course is confidential, you are people of the police. His name isn't Mannheim. Kassel. A long time ago—SS Colonel Konrad Kassel, stationed at Auschwitz and involved in the murders of sixty thousand—"

A sharp knock on the entrance door.

"Come in," called Lieutenant Parker.

The policeman, Brody. A typewritten sheet in his hand. He gave it to the lieutenant.

"Thank you."

Brody went out, closing the door softly.

The lieutenant's eyes scanned the sheet; he looked up to McGregor, and then to her. "All right. Where is he?"

"Gone."

"What've we got?" McGregor asked, quite mildly.

"One hundred percent on the .22. If she took that gun off him, he's our baby. Did you, Miss Gaza?"

"I did."

"Where is he, Miss Gaza?"

"Gone. Out of your country. On his way for a visit in my country."

"The hell." He flung the typewritten sheet to the desk. It fluttered, and subsided.

"Lieutenant," she said, "you want him for one murder, we want him for sixty thousand murders. Which way does the preference lie?"

"The lady has a point," McGregor said.

"Thank you, Mr. McGregor," she said. "And thank you for much more. And perhaps, pragmatically, I shall be of help to you in your business. Because there will be full appreciation from my government. When my report is written, not I, not Dave Jordan, but you shall emerge the shining knight, the paladin, and deservedly."

"Maybe not." The inscrutable blue eyes, smiling at the corners, were full upon her, and held her like a vise. There was a feeling of release, physical relief, when he turned them from her and looked toward Lieutenant Parker. "All right," he said.

Parker touched a lever of the intercom.

"Let's have him," he said.

Before she was ready, not yet prepared, before she could inquire, a side door opened and Dave Jordan, two policemen behind him, stood in the doorway.

"Dave!"

What had gone wrong? She was on her feet.

"Not Dave," McGregor said.

"Dave Jordan."

"Not Dave Jordan," McGregor said. "Walter Harbin."

ℜ Thirty-three

TALL, dark, wan, motionless in the doorway, he smiled. What had gone wrong?

"Dave—the trunk?"

"Delivered. On its way."

"I believe I can confirm that," McGregor said.

"Dave! Anna?"

"And all her luggage. Delivered. On their way."

"If Anna's a small woman with a patch on her forehead, I believe I can confirm that too," McGregor said.

"Dave! What . . . ?"

"Not Dave," McGregor said. "Walter Harbin."

"Not Dave," said the man in the doorway. A smile again, a little nod, somehow gallant. "They'll tell you. All. I've told them." A shrug. "It was nice, Julie." He turned away. The policemen took him. The door swung shut.

She whirled around to McGregor.

"What! What the *hell!*"

" 'Commit a crime,' said Ralph Waldo Emerson, 'and the earth is made of glass.' "

"Here we go," murmured Parker.

" 'Some damning circumstance always transpires,' said R. W. Emerson. For Walter Harbin, I transpired. I was the damning circumstance. Please sit down, Miss Gaza."

She remained standing.

Parker clicked a lever of the intercom. "Bring in the satchel."

"Walter Harbin," McGregor said. "When I saw him in your hotel suite, I remembered him. I've a rather retentive memory."

"Retentive," Parker said. "Like a steel trap. Like a camera, a motion picture camera, the film inside his head. Photographic."

"Walter Harbin," McGregor said. "A sporty fella, a high liver, but one of the shrewdest and most successful confidence men in the business. Never convicted, but several times arrested. The last time here in New York, about ten years ago. We had him in the line-up. Line-up. The spotlight's on them, we're in the dark. They can't see us when we see them. I saw Walter Harbin."

A knock on the side door.

"Come in," Parker called.

She recognized the plaid-patterned suitcase.

"Right here," Parker said and pointed.

The policeman laid it on the desk and went out.

McGregor said, "Do sit down, Miss Gaza."

She sat. She did not cross her legs. She tugged at her skirt.

"Walter Harbin," McGregor said. "New York born, but an international figure, suave, smooth, a linguist. Last we heard of him he was in South America, Buenos Aires. But then there he is in your suite in the Delmonico and you introduce him as Dave Jordan, your fiancé. I was very much interested because by then I knew about a loose million bucks—the Ludwig Lubeck business. A loose million bucks, that sure would explain Walter Harbin's presence. How he had become Dave Jordan, how he had got that close to you that you were introducing him as your fiancé—that I did not know. But I stayed with him. I wasn't prying into your affairs. His affairs. I hope you understand that, Miss Gaza."

"Yes."

"I stayed with him. He was stalking Mannheim at the bank, I was stalking him. I saw Mannheim come this afternoon, carrying"—he pointed—"that plaid bag. I saw Walter Harbin—your Dave Jordan—take him, you at the wheel of the station wagon, watched you drive back to the hotel. Walter Harbin came out, the plaid bag came out, a trunk came out. Mannheim didn't. I have a vague suspicion"—the blue eyes twinkled—"of what was contained in the trunk. Not my business. Walter Harbin was my business, the plaid bag a part of that business; the trunk, none of my business. I should like to tell you this now, on behalf of Walter Harbin. He's made a full confession—we've got him dead to rights and he's wise enough to know the value of voluntary confession in mitigation at the time of sentencing—but he told us nothing about the trunk. When we asked him about Mannheim, he said he'd left him upstairs with you, said he was interested in the contents of the plaid bag, nothing else. Rather splendid of him, don't you think, Miss Gaza?"

"Yes."

"He'll probably crack under hot interrogation, but so far it hasn't been hot, and so this thief—and murderer—has been rather splendid." He lit a cigarette. "Anyway, we tailed him to Seventieth Street, watched him pick up the little lady with the patch, tailed him to Kennedy, made our inquiries while they were passing the stuff through Customs. Israeli, a government plane, which was fine and okay with me. Whatever was to be delivered he was delivering, but he wouldn't deliver himself or the plaid bag—and he didn't. When the plane taxied off, we took him."

"Dave Jordan." She shook her head. "Walter Harbin?"

178

"Lieutenant Parker and I, we checked it out. Your fiancé, among other things in his wallet—he had a newspaper clipping from a Buenos Aires paper that Walter Harbin was dead, a suicide. We checked it out. Walter Harbin in Buenos Aires *was* dead, a suicide."

"I—I don't understand."

"Neither," grunted Parker, "the hell did we."

"Because Walter Harbin was very much alive, right here in our custody. We put the Buenos Aires cops onto it, and stayed along with them, which is why I wasn't calling back on any of my telephone messages. They disinterred the body. A mess. Upper part of the torso entirely smashed, unrecognizable, a head-first leap down twenty-two stories, and upstairs a typewritten suicide note. But the hands were not smashed, and the fingers were good enough for prints. There we were lucky. They had comparisons. Walter Harbin had done a short haul in the army down there, his prints were on file. So were Dave Jordan's who had done a short haul with a twelve-year-old who looked sixteen. Statutory rape. Sentence suspended, but prints on file. The dead man was not Walter Harbin. The dead man was Dave Jordan. So instead of a closed file on suicide, they had an open file on murder."

"But we close up their file," said Parker, "because we have got their murderer, thanks to the Inspector's photographic memory."

"But how?" she said. "How?"

McGregor sighed. "Harbin filled us in on all of it. His defense down there will be self-defense, and he *might* make it stick. But if they don't get him there on the murder, we've got him here on the larceny—grand larceny. Anyway, he gave us a full confession, voluntary. He says you know most of it, but know it in reverse, that is from the viewpoint of the supposed Dave Jordan, the role Harbin was playing for you."

"Yes, but I still don't understand. I—"

"Harbin, an accomplished swindler, was doing all right in South America. He had got himself well entrenched with the National Socialist League, and was picking up money not only from Dave Jordan but from other agents. Buenos Aires in Argentina, like Lisbon in Portugal, is a hotbed of international espionage. For Jordan, at three hundred a week, he was digging up information on Mannheim.

"Then, as he told you, he learned about Lubeck, Lubeck's connection with Mannheim, and the million bucks cached up here in the United States, and the fact that Lubeck was coming up to join Mannheim. Manheim, then, was the focus. On that aspect, he told you the truth. He did invite Jordan to his place, a twenty-second floor penthouse, and did proposition him. They would work together on Mannheim and Lubeck, take over at the right moment, and split a million dollars between them. Although he realized the risk he put on the full pressure—blackmail. By his own devices—and Harbin's devices are many—he knew exactly who Dave Jordan was, a Shinbet agent and not a free-lance writer with a small independent income. And he told him. Knowing the risk, he told him. He felt he had the best of all aces in the hole. Cupidity. He was offering a fifty-fifty split of a million bucks.

"Miss Gaza, you, certainly, know the three alternatives of an exposed agent—exposed to one such as Walter Harbin. He either has to quit his job, or go along with his blackmailer, or—"

Flatly she said, "Kill."

"Harbin knew his risk, he was ready. He lost. Jordan attacked. But he was no match for Walter Harbin, an expert at karate. When it was over, Dave Jordan was dead with a broken neck. And Harbin, ever resourceful, came to a quick decision. He didn't want a murder on his hands, and he did want to get up to the States. They were of rather similar appearance, he and Jordan, of similar age, both slim, dark, rather good looking. He changed clothes with Jordan, switching effects contained in the clothes. He typed the suicide note. He carried him to a rear window, dropped him out head first. Twenty-two stories. There would be no face. Identification would be by effects. The note upstairs would make it clearly suicide. Then quickly he went out by a back way, walked a few streets, took a cab across town to Jordan's apartment. He holed in there, packing. Using Jordan's passport and credentials, he would come up to the States as Dave Jordan. The next morning he received a cable, decided to go along with it, play it by ear. You know the rest."

"I don't get it," Parker said. Nobody answered him. He opened a drawer of his desk, took out a yellow slip of paper. "Cablegram," he said and stood up and brought it around to her.

RETURN NEW YORK IMMEDIATELY. REPORT RABIN AT
CONSULATE. GAZA WILL CONTACT. YAGID.

"What I mean, Miss Gaza. Shinbet. Don't you the hell *know*
whom you're working with?"

"Not always."

"That's what I mean. I don't get it."

"Are you being naïve, Lieutenant?"

"Am I?" He put the yellow slip on the desk, flattened it with
the palm of his hand.

"Shinbet is massive, complex, mesh within mesh. Take your
own CIA. Think about that, Lieutenant. Many operatives—
hundreds upon hundreds—most of whom don't know one another. We of Shinbet—like your people of CIA—get our orders
from a central source. Assigned to one another, frequently the
agents are perfect strangers."

"Yeah," he grunted. "Sorry. That's me. Naïve." He retrieved the
stump of his cigar from the edge of an ashtray.

"Well, that's about it." McGregor patted his knees, stood up,
smiled toward her. "Kept you past your bedtime, Miss Gaza?"

"No!" she answered quickly, too quickly. And softened it. "I'm
sort of a night person, Mr. McGregor." She went to the plaid bag
on the desk, tried the locks, they were open. She laid back the
cover.

"Something?" Parker said. "A million bucks. Ever look right
square down at a million dollars, Miss Gaza? Me, never. It's
something to tell your kids about."

"Me never either, before today. Today, twice. This is my
second time."

"Got kids to tell?"

"No kids. Now what happens to it, Lieutenant?"

"Goes back by legal channels. Where it belongs. To the National Socialist League of Argentina."

"Paradox," she said.

"Pardon?" he said.

"Shinbet," she said. "They're the enemy down there, that
League. Yet it's Shinbet responsible for the return of a million
dollars. If not for Shinbet, Mannheim and Lubeck would have got

181

away with it. Funny? Shinbet doing a job for the League. Paradox?"

"Yeah, I never thought of it that way."

"Laughter in the alehouse," McGregor said.

"Here we go again," Parker said.

"Laughter?" she said to McGregor. "Alehouse?"

"Shakespeare put it in Desdemona's mouth: 'These are old fond paradoxes to make fools laugh in the alehouse.' "

"Parables," Parker said.

"Oh?" she said brightly. Sprightly. "Parables?"

"I know the guy, Miss Gaza. A lifetime. Even when he quotes, the Inspector speaks in parables." He plunged the cigar at his teeth and grinned around it, biting down, crookedly. "You wish interpretation?"

"Cut it, Louie."

"I wish indeed."

"Alehouse? The whole world. Fools? You, me, he, Mannheim, Jordan, Harbin—everybody. Drinkers in the alehouse, we must all in the end laugh at the old fond paradoxes. But the laughter, in the end, is bitter."

"His interpretation entirely," McGregor said. "My dear friend the lieutenant, poet, philosopher, pessimist."

Parker took the cigar out of his mouth, looked at his watch.

"Late. I'll have one of my boys take you home in a squad car, Miss Gaza."

"I'll take Miss Gaza home." To her: "If I may?"

"Well, thank you, sir."

"Good night, Louie."

"Night."

"Good night, Lieutenant."

Night. Starry. Springtime night. Moon. A soft little breeze, warm, pleasant. They walked. She held his arm. Hard. Like a rock. It was good, walking in springtime night. It was over. Job done, accomplished. Variations on the theme. A million dollars but in essence, minor. Dave Jordan who was not Dave Jordan, minor. Major was Anna Stryker, on her way. Major was Mannheim, Konrad Kassel, on his way. There would be furor, possibly extradition. Not her affair. For the statesmen, the politicians, the lawyers. If he were extradited to Germany for the trial, still good. The world publicity would make for a fair trial, despite the League, the Blue Group, his powerful allies. Not her affair. Job done. A few loose ends to be gathered and she would go home. Perhaps a short vacation. And then a new assignment. But now, here, for her it was over, and now here walking in the starry night it was pure, personal. And they walked, quite silently. And then a cab. And she sat, purposely, very near him, thigh to thigh. Felt him. His warmth. God, he must feel me. Warmth. I will invite him up for a drink. I will make no mention of the balance of his fee, give him no proper excuse. Will he accept? In the middle of the night, a drink. Of itself a kind of assignation. A woman alone. The subtle implication of a hotel suite. Middle of the night. Invitation for a drink. Will he accept?

Michael Innes

AN AWKWARD LIE
Bobby, son of that great master of detection Sir John Appleby, finds a body on a golf course. As he wonders what to do, a very attractive girl arrives. When Bobby returns after calling the police, however, the girl has gone . . . and so has the corpse.

CANDLESHOE
What mysterious treasure lies hidden in the dark heart of Candleshoe Manor? Is it bullion from the Spanish Main? Priceless paintings from Venice? And what breath-catching adventures will unfold before the riddle of the treasure is finally, excitingly solved?

FROM *LONDON* FAR
A random scrap of Augustan poetry muttered in a tobacconist's shop thrusts an absent-minded scholar through a trapdoor into short-lived leadership of London's biggest art racket. Then it's a chase along a twisting trail of Titians and Giottos, of violence and sudden fear. . . .

HAMLET, REVENGE!
The Lord Chancellor is shot in the midst of a private performance of *Hamlet*. Behind the scenes there are thirty-one suspects; in the audience, twenty-seven. "Suspicions," says Appleby of Scotland Yard, "crowd thick and fast upon us."

MONEY FROM HOLME
A brilliant young painter dies in a foreign revolution . . . then returns from the dead. But numerous members of the art world emerge to send him back again.

THE MYSTERIOUS COMMISSION
Tempted by the offer of a huge fee, artist Charles Honeybath accepts a strange assignment: paint the portrait of an unnamed man in an unnamed place. Is it all a trick of some sort? Or does the portrait have a sinister meaning of its own?

WHAT HAPPENED AT HAZELWOOD
Spend a weekend in the English countryside—old quarrels revived, unbridled sex . . . and murder all over the place!

Geoffrey Household

RED ANGER

A young English clerk fakes his own suicide to escape a boring job—then reappears as a Roumanian refugee from a Russian trawler fleet. But from the moment Adrian Gurney, alias Ionel Petrescu, is "discovered" on the coast, he is caught in a sinister and unexpected intrigue: He is recruited to hunt down Alwyn Rory, fugitive and reputed traitor. Gurney manages to locate Rory's hiding place, and the two soon find themselves on the run together, as the C.I.A., the K.G.B., and MI5 close in.

ROGUE MALE

His mission was revenge, and revenge means assassination. In return he'll be cruelly tortured, tracked by secret agents, followed by the police, relentlessly pursued by a ruthless killer. They'll hunt him like a wild beast, and to survive he'll have to think and live like a rogue male. "A tale of adventure, suspense, even mystery, for whose sheer thrilling quality one may seek long to find a parallel . . . and in its sparse, tense, desperately alive narrative it will keep, long after the last page is finished, its hold from the first page on the reader's mind" —*The New York Times Book Review*.

WATCHER IN THE SHADOWS

Watcher in the Shadows is the story of a manhunt, of a protracted duel fought out in London and the English countryside by two of the most accomplished and deadly intelligence officers to have survived World War II. One of them is a Viennese who served in the British Intelligence; the other is a dangerous fanatic who has already murdered three men. "A thriller of the highest quality"—Anthony Boucher, *The New York Times Book Review*.

More Mysteries from Penguin